"The tragedy of identity is something I can relate to. Every day, we juggle a confident public persona with our private anxieties."

- Ligeia Gordon

"We are who we are, not who our parents were. Unfortunately, destiny doesn't see things that way."

- Morris Quint

"One should always have something sensational to read on the train. I think I'll stick with Agatha Christie."

- The Author's Mother

FIRST EDITION

ISBN: 978 1083 172211

Cover image by Alexander Baidin

Lost Lady

a novel

by

Michael Reidy

Lattimer & Co.

PHILADELPHIA·LONDON·PARIS

2019

For four Valentines

The glory of man consists in the fact that he is a distinct creation, an individuality without counterpart in the universe. The development of this personality is his mission; if he does it well, his face will show it, and if he does ill, no art can hide it.

- Andrew O'Connor, Jr, sculptor, first foreign winner of the Prix d'Or, Paris Salon, 1928

Lost Lady

Prologue
The Prophecy

Paris
November 1920

No one in Paris questions the appropriateness of couples. Fat men and thin women; short men with tall women; handsome men with very plain women. The last thing that would be questioned in Paris is older men with young women.

The sculptor and the young girl, perhaps not yet twenty, attracted no attention as they walked across the Pont Mirabeau towards the Quai d'Arteuil.

Nearing sixty, he walked with a straight elegance accented by his good, but old, fur-trimmed coat, keeping his head erect even in the face of the wind that rushed down the river. With his polished stick and nearly new leather gloves, he brought a lingering touch of the *fin de siècle* into the new world.

Dwarfed by his height, mass and sheer presence, the girl trotted to keep up with his strides, her head bent, and her hands bare (Russians seldom wear gloves), clutching her too thin coat.

They walked on, then turned into the Avenue de

Versailles and approached the door to Number 73.

It was not unusual for M. Hébrard to be at his *atelier*, but he was just as often to be found at his gallery in Rue Royale. After pleasantries and the offer of coffee, the three proceeded from the small office into the foundry.

"We have the wax models ready for your inspection," M. Hébrard said.

The sculptor inspected three identical wax busts made from a mould of his plaster *maquette*. He spent nearly ten minutes scrutinising each one as M. Hébrard and the model sat on stools next to the bench.

"It's a wonderful likeness," observed M. Hébrard to the girl who still clutched her coat around her, even though the room was very warm from the furnace.

The girl continued to gaze at the busts but said nothing.

The sculptor spoke quietly to one of the craftsmen who made small adjustments, chasing the wax, then inspected where he had scratched his name in the *maquette* at the base of the neck to ensure that the letters were clear. He also took out his glass to read the founder's mark, though he knew Hébrard would have checked this as soon as the wax model had been removed from the mould. Like the seal from a signet ring, the square mark with rounded corners was clear: *Cire Perdue A. A. Hébrard* was stamped, centred on three lines. He nodded and quietly thanked the artisan.

The inside of the wax bust was then filled with a thick mixture that would set hard. This investment would be removed once the bronze was cast.

The sculptor stood back and watched as the foundryman then appeared to disfigure the bust, so carefully prepared, by fixing round bars of wax leading upwards to a bulbous cup. The men looked on in satisfaction and chatted in low voices while the girl looked puzzled but asked nothing.

"All is in order," Hébrard said after inspecting the gates and vents. "We can proceed."

The artisan carried the prepared bust to the furnace followed by the sculptor, M. Hébrard and the girl. The sculptor now removed his coat and hung it on a peg and put on a heavy apron. Hébrard did the same, but the girl remained by the wall, clutching her coat.

Over the next hour, the wax model was dipped in layers of slurry and sand until it was wholly unrecognisable. It was then placed in a bowl-like metal container and supported with wooden wedges and sand until it was stable. The heat in the room had increased as the level of the furnace was brought up so the bronze was smooth.

As the impurities were skimmed off the top of the crucible, Hébrard said to the girl, "The bronze will melt the wax and replace it. *La dame de cire sera perdue et la dame de bronze restera.* The lady of wax will be lost and the lady of bronze will remain."

She stared at the glowing crucible as it was brought towards the mould.

"*Et moi?*" she said, her voice stronger and richer than expected. "*Je vais devenir la dame perdue.*"

The sculptor spoke to her gently.

"No, my dear," he said. "You are the lucky one. Monsieur and I will be forgotten, but your beauty will last for hundreds, if not a thousand years."

The girl looked at him without affection or anger, then returned her gaze to the crucible where the bronze was being poured.

"*Je voudrais bien être la dame perdue,*" she said. "I would like to be the lost lady. To disappear; that is why I left Russia."

With the pour finished, the men set down the crucible and took off their gloves. One of them wiped his brow.

The sculptor walked up to them, shook their hands and thanked them.

"We should have it in the gallery by the end of next week," Hébrard said. "Unless you'd like to inspect it here first."

"I'll let you work your magic, Adrien," the sculptor said, well aware of the reputation of Fonderie Hébrard for finishing and applying the desired patina. "I'll send some bases around."

"*Bien. Au revoir, mon ami,*" Hébrard said, then turned to the girl. "*Je ne pense pas que vous resterez à toujours perdue.* I do not think you will remain lost forever."

Foreword

For a long time, I had no idea what to do with my father's recollections. I found them among his business day books and files when clearing his office. They were in his old-school copperplate hand and though perfectly legible in their hard covered notebooks, it was nearly a decade before I read them and a further decade before I decided to publish them.

I've re-read them several times; what was difficult to decide was whether he intended them to be published, or if they were just for himself and family. I don't suppose they reveal anything that isn't by now widely known. However, from time to time, he seems to be talking to a reader, and that reader doesn't seem to be specifically me.

Solange Alexandra Boivet
Paris

I

Explanation

It was never my intention to write about my life, especially about a part of my life that has so little in common with today's world. Indeed, it is hard to believe that these things ever happened at all, let alone to me. While age enables one to be more subjective and philosophical about events, it also means one tends to be more selective and, perhaps, too forgiving.

My story reads more like a fantasy today because the society in which these events took place is so remote. However, there are still some things to be learned from the dinosaurs while one or two of us are still around who remember *les années folles* and some of the personalities who made it what it was.

This book is both a way to record my experiences of those years and to help me make more sense of them. Everyone mentioned is now dead. I am nearly eighty years old, but have had the time to collect such agenda, notes and memorabilia that I still possess, and also to spend time in the libraries to research information that was not available until recently.

The best I can do is arrange these islands of memory

in chronological order. There are a few passages of pure imagination, but they are based on what I was told. The only other voice is that of the young lady I knew as Natasha, and as you will discover, her effect on my experience of the 1920s was considerable.

In February 1921, I was living in Paris. I had begun to work at Moreau, Doré & Cie., a firm of grain powder brokers. It sounds boring, and I suppose it was, but at the time it was all the excitement I could handle. It had taken me nearly two years to get to the point where I felt I could go out to get any sort of work at all. Even those without injuries and who had never been near the front were wounded.

Those wounds made forgetting imperative, but it was very hard on those who were unprepared, or unable, to forget. While soldiers came back from World War II as heroes, they did not from Vietnam or Algeria, and I can see the Americans now returning from Vietnam facing the same lack of understanding.

On returning to this normality, I made fairly rapid progress in some aspects of my life, while others remained impeded. One of the areas where I had made good progress was in developing a curiosity – even a hunger – to see what was going on in the new, post-horror world. While much of it struck me as a way for people to distract themselves from the pain and loss of the war, other things struck me as wholly new and exciting.

II

The Model

Art, music and dance had come to the fore in Paris before the war and now seemed to be enjoying an unbridled exuberance with undreamt of sights and sounds seducing, appeasing, assaulting and confounding the senses. In spite of the constructed gaiety, the peace was mournful and even I could see people were doing whatever they could to forget. Noise, dissonant music, drinking too many exotic concoctions, having casual sex and spouting literary, political or philosophical tosh to forget Jacque, Henri or Bill who was gone; that the world they knew was gone. The Tsar was dead, and someone named Warren G. Harding had just become President of the United States of America.

It was February and I had made myself go to an opening at Galerie Hébrard in the Rue Royale. Only the thinnest veneer of this exhibition opening made it anything like those before the world fell apart. Some of the old crowd were still there, dressed in their twenty-year-old formality, talking to each other quietly, but no doubt just as damning as the younger *aficionados* and the perennial students. The students looked the same as ever: gaunt, hungry, hairy, threadbare and hiding behind brave bold words and half-formed thoughts. The same students had challenged and mocked painters and sculptors before the war, even as they had baited Caravaggio.

Still, gallery owners and artists tolerated them because their judgements, though often wrong, were honest, unlike the sycophants and financiers who promoted anyone whose work was new or cheap, so they could ride the coat-tails made large through their patronage. Now the students were marked with experience; their studies interrupted, their futures blighted; many had themselves come back from the trenches to occupy the hard, unforgiving seats of the lecture hall and revel in the drudgery of reading ancient texts that were supposed to speak to the new age.

To me, it seemed that it wasn't only the people that were shattered and scarred by the war, but so was the sculpture that was presented here. All of it shared the fine casting and patina that Atelier Hébrard was noted for, but the disparity of the work was more evident than ever: Pompon, Bourdell, O'Connor, Maillol, and even two pieces by the tragic Rembrandt Bugatti. While the shows immediately after the Armistice clung to previous standards of taste, this one betrayed the coming revolutions in art and society that the war and civil unrest had brought.

I moved from piece to piece, giving each a considered

scrutiny from all angles before moving to the next. I had been largely oblivious to the people about me until I finished regarding a tortured bronze at the edge of the room when, while moving towards the next, found myself staring at a young girl, who stood against the wall looking lost and fearful.

I suppose I had been regarding her as a statue for some time when she turned and looked directly at me startling me back to reality.

"I think it rude to stare," she said in heavily accented French.

While having been confronted by more surprising moments, the young lady's directness caused me to blush in embarrassment.

"I am very sorry, mam'selle," I stammered. "I was somewhere else."

"I am neither on show, nor for sale," she said, not meanly, almost flirtatiously.

I continued to look at her, about to give another superficial comment, for I wanted to explain myself but without apologising. Then, I stopped.

"I've met you already."

The girl regarded me with curiosity.

"Over there," I said, waving vaguely to a grouping of statues in a far corner. "There's a bust of you, isn't there?"

She seemed pleased that I had recognised her.

"Now," I ventured, "the question is, are you someone famous or an artist's model?"

She looked amused; I was struck by how thin and hungry looking she was.

"Can't I be both?" she asked, and I laughed, perhaps too loudly.

I wanted to keep her attention before she concluded I was a fool not worth knowing.

"Don't move," I instructed her, and moved through the hoard to where I thought I'd seen her bust.

The statue was not quite where I thought it was, so it took several minutes before I found it and made my way back to where I had left the girl.

She hadn't moved.

Her face held the same expression it had when I first saw her. It didn't change when she spoke.

"So, am I someone famous, or just an artist's model?" she posed.

"I don't know," I said. "Your bust is entitled *Madame X*."

She gave me an enigmatic look, such as she wore in the bust.

"The question is, was that your choice of name, or the sculptor's?" I asked.

"Does it matter?"

"Oh, yes!" I exclaimed, intrigued to see how far I could

push her. "If it was yours, then you are concealing something. If it was the sculptor's title, then he is the one playing games, and we are supposed to think the bust is of someone significant. Possibly so he can attract more commissions from people who think they are important, too."

The girl laughed and her whole being seemed to brighten.

"If I wanted to conceal my identity, why would I have modelled for a bust that would be so publicly displayed?" she asked.

Her voice intrigued me almost more than her appearance. In spite of her thin frame and wispy look, her voice was full, and rich. What was the accent? Polish? Russian? Some Eastern European language? I didn't know.

Following several only partially successful attempts at conversation, I tried a different approach and offered to buy her a meal. I wouldn't be able to afford much, but I guessed that I could afford more than she could.

"And, you? Do *you* have a name?" she asked.

"Charles Boivet."

Madame X nodded and appeared satisfied.

"Very well," she said and waited to be led from the gallery.

The bistro I had in mind was a ten-minute walk away, and I was afraid that she would change her mind after walking a few hundred metres. She did not, and then surprised me when a little more than halfway to our destination, she took my arm.

We said little, and pulled our coats close in the chill evening. Occasionally, she would stop and look in a window. Sometimes it was antiques; sometimes clothes; but it was always expensive.

Somewhere along the line this girl had acquired either good taste or an eye for what was valuable. Either way, I thought she would be interesting if I could get her to talk.

This "Madame X" seemed unlike the girls her age I knew, but what had made her that way, I couldn't imagine. I guessed she was from some place in Eastern Europe, or beyond, and there had been horrors that a young lady might wish to escape from.

I began to wonder if this was folly as my attempts to make conversation had not elicited much response. Asking her about what she looked at in the shop windows was more successful; she was more comfortable talking about those things than about herself.

We stood outside a large shop that looked as though it hadn't been tidied for a century with a motley assortment of furniture and light-fittings, filling every patch of floor, wall and ceiling. I hoped she might reveal something more if carefully questioned.

The girl seemed lost in the tangle of chairs and dressers, mirrors and lamps.

"What's the most interesting thing you see?" I asked.

She gave no indication that she had heard me but continued to stare into the depths of the shop. When I was about to prompt her either for an answer or to move on, she spoke.

"Our reflections in the window," she said, then smiled to herself.

ॐ

We reached the bistro I knew in a small street behind the opera. I was greeted by name and a gratifying fuss was made over the girl. It was still early enough that the performance had not yet finished, and tables were available. Soon it would fill with those who could only afford the cheaper seats with the gods and stage hands who came regularly; dressers, make-up artists and musicians all frequented *Le Livre de Vie* if they were not in a café living on drink.

We were shown to a table on the side wall but near the window. I let the girl have the place where she could look out. A waiter handed us menus and she began reading, but before opening mine, I looked at her and asked:

"What's your name? I can't go on calling you 'Madame X.'"

"Why not? It suits me."

"Not really," I contradicted gently. "'Mam'selle X', perhaps."

She smiled again. When she did, she almost looked pretty. When she did not, she looked interesting.

"What would you like to eat?"

She closed the menu.

"You choose for me."

"Very well. Red or white wine?"

I hoped to get a clue to her preference, but she gave her slight smile again.

"You can call me Natasha," she said.

"Is that your real name?"

"The wine depends on what you order for me," she said.

The waiter came, and I ordered a *poisson Saint Pierre* for Natasha and a *pavé* for myself. For wine I asked for a *demi* of the *cuvée du patron*, red and white.

"Natasha is as much my name as Madame X," she said, but this time I thought she was teasing me.

"Paris is full of Mesdames X," I replied. "There's Sargent's, Rodin's, O'Connor's, the one we saw tonight, and I don't know how many more."

"You go to a lot of galleries," she laughed. "There are quite a few Natashas, too."

The wine arrived, and I poured her a glass. As I poured mine, I ventured:

"Will you tell me something of this Natasha?"

"The *poisson Saint Pierre* was a good choice."

She drank her wine and gazed out the window. I nibbled a piece of bread as I watched her. She was taller than average, and her boots made her taller still, and I thought she was very thin. She wore several layers of clothes, so it was difficult to tell. Her auburn hair was full and pinned and piled seemingly wherever she could make it stay, even so, several locks appeared to be perpetually out of place.

She suddenly turned to face me, catching me off guard. I began to apologise for staring.

"I am a model and used to being stared at," she said. "I am also used to being ignored."

She said it with a resignation that unexpectedly moved me; no person this young should ever feel this way. What had made her feel so alone? It must have been traumatic, and I doubted she'd reveal anything this evening.

Although foreign, her French was impeccable, if a little formal and old fashioned.

"Why are you looking so sad, Charles?" she asked.

"Only because I thought you looked unhappy."

She gave a smile and her eyes radiated a warmth I hadn't seen.

"This is one of the best evenings I've had since coming to Paris," she exclaimed brightly. "I've had my head exhibited at a gallery, and I've been taken to dinner by a prominent young man."

She spoke without irony, and the aura of despair lifted. I looked into her eyes in an attempt to fathom something about her. Anything.

"When did you come to Paris?"

She looked down.

"I didn't mean to pry – "

She looked at me, but her face gave nothing away.

"No, it's all right. My life has been – ," she stopped and reconsidered what she was about to say. "I came when I was quite young, in 1909. I lived with an aunt and uncle – at least that's what I called them – and went to school. My uncle had some friends who were artists and they started drawing me. I've modelled for many artists – most of them bad, but a few good ones, or at least interesting."

"Does that keep you busy?"

"It keeps me busy, but it doesn't pay well," she said. "It's often boring, unless the artist talks to me or has a visitor. When I was younger, many of the great artists would visit. When I posed for Degas, Rodin would come sometimes. M. Hébrard casts for him and through him and Degas, I'd meet others and get more work."

"Were your aunt and uncle there tonight?" I asked.

Her face darkened.

"They both died in the epidemic in 1918," she said

softly. "They weren't old. It was after they died that I had to look after myself."

"You weren't very old yourself," I said.

"I was fifteen."

She ate some bread quietly and took a full drink of the wine.

"I also work for Mme Goncharova when the Ballet Russes is in Paris," she said, seeming to cheer up. "She does the costumes and I help with fittings and repairs. That's fun but doesn't pay well either."

The food arrived, and I refilled her glass and watched her eyes as she looked at the fish, potatoes, and petits pois with pearl onions. She paused until the waiter left and then looked at me for the cue to begin. I noticed her manners, her hands, and the length of her fingers as she picked up her knife and fork. Though her hands were very thin, they were fine, and her long fingers had well-cared for, if short, nails.

While we ate, I told her a little about myself. How my university years had been interrupted by the war, and how I'd always enjoyed the museums and galleries. About my exciting job, I said as little as possible.

"Are you from Paris?" she asked.

"My father has a small business in Montmirail, about eight kilometres from Paris.

Natasha laughed when I mentioned grain powder

brokering.

"You can make money doing that?" she asked, incredulously.

"Oh, yes," I said. "We don't trade flour, but other sorts of grain powders, mostly for industrial purposes."

She giggled.

"I'm always amazed at the jobs people do," she said. "At Madame Duflot's you hear of – "

I froze, fork in mid-air, at the mention of Mme Duflot. My stomach dropped and I went cold. I tried to collect myself as unobtrusively as possible; put my fork down, and wiped my mouth in desperate stage-business waiting for Natasha to continue. For even in my inexperience, I knew that Mme Duflot's was one of the best known "houses" in Paris.

☙

I had seen enough of human nature and death not to be surprised by much, but I had not grown so cynical as not to be shocked to learn that this young girl was in the employ of a legendary and select Parisian brothel. I confess to feeling conspicuous and suddenly believing that everyone around was watching us. Instinctively, I glanced around the restaurant.

Disconcertingly, Natasha laughed quite loudly.

"Poor Charles," she said. "Your face! Indeed, it does not surprise me that you are surprised, but one must live."

She paused, then noting my confusion, continued.

"I play the piano," she said. "I saw you looking at my fingers. I have a long reach for a woman, but not the strength to play in the concert hall. I have played all my life, and Mme Duflot has an excellent piano, a gentlemanly clientele, and I assure you – though why I should since it is none of your business – I do not 'entertain' except with my playing."

It took time for me to absorb this. I drank some wine and refilled our glasses. Then I picked up my fork.

"And what composers do you favour?" I asked.

She laughed again.

"Dear Charles! Such a gentleman," she said. "Like all pianists, I love Chopin and Tchaikovsky and I would love to give a recital of Rachmaninoff, Prokofiev, and Ravel. Though, there is much beauty in Debussy and Fauré. I think we will hear more of them."

"And Stravinsky?"

She laughed.

"Oh, yes! We shall certainly hear *much* more of *him*, whether we wish to or not! Of course, most of what I have to play at Mme Duflot's are old songs and sometimes new ones."

I continued to feel awkward for the rest of the evening, but Natasha picked up the initiative, asking questions about my work, the places I'd visited, and my favourite places in Paris. She had the sense not to ask about my experiences in the war.

I realised during our exchange that for her, I didn't really matter. I could be anyone; she was not about to have her evening spoiled. She had seen a bronze of herself in a renowned gallery with a price tag that would take her many years to earn.

Watching her devouring her fish and potatoes, it wasn't hard to see what had attracted the artists to her. There was elegance, but there was also the hint of presumption. She didn't exactly sulk, but there was a detachment that seemed to separate her from reality. Maybe that's what the artists liked: that partially hidden, haunted quality.

I had seen enough of educated and polite society to recognise both characteristics in Natasha. The way she handled her knife and fork were foreign but of a refined manner, born of habit, not affectation. The way she held her wine glass and drank were similarly studied, yet fluid and gracious. These refinements jarred with her obvious poverty; the Bohemian disorder of her hair and the almost thoughtless way in which she applied her make-up; these were not affectations but either a sign of her changed conditions, or a carefully calculated illusion to mislead.

She stopped eating to look at me again. I began to

apologise once more for staring.

"Don't, Charles," she said quietly. "Being stared at is little enough to give for your kindness and this good meal."

I laughed, not only at what she said, but more at the unconscious style of *noblesse oblige* in which she said it. I ordered coffee; Natasha requested a cup of tea and asked for a dish of jam with it. The waiter displayed no reaction, but I was fascinated to watch her stir a spoonful of it into her tea.

Too quickly, we finished and Natasha looked at the clock on the wall.

"I must go soon," she said. "I need to be there to play when the best patrons come in."

"I'm sorry you have to go there," I said, fully aware of how priggish it sounded.

She laughed gently, not mocking me.

"Believe me, Charles, tonight I shall speak with cabinet ministers, chief inspectors, millionaires and bankers. Often, it's how I get my engagements to pose," she said easily, then she looked at him seriously.

"Charles, you have seen much pain and suffering, and so have I. Can we really condemn a little pleasure?"

I noted she hadn't said "innocent pleasure," but she was right about what I had seen, and I wondered what her own experience had been.

"We shouldn't be careless with life, but neither should we be so cautious that we fail to live," she said. "You know what Tolstoy said – "

She broke off suddenly and was silent for a moment. Then she looked at the clock again.

"I must go," she said. "Come escort me to the Rue Fonchart. I won't make you take me to the door."

III

Distractions

Back in my room, I couldn't settle. I had changed for bed, but was wide awake trying to resolve questions about Natasha and fathom the contradictions she presented. I put more coal on the small fire and sat in my dressing gown in the only comfortable chair and tried to read.

Not many nineteen-year-old Russian girls in Paris could quote Tolstoy – or knew who he was. That confirmed my supposition that she was well-bred, but where was her family? She'd been in Paris since before the revolution, so was not a refugee. An émigré? I looked for an explanation that would draw together her supposed background, education, the poverty and the fatalism she seemed to embody. All right, she was Russian, and used to the idea of being a slave of destiny, and she did seem to have fit rather a lot into a very short life. Might she not be as young as she looked? She was thin and pale enough to look very young, but might she be older? She was certainly not intimidated by the gallery or the restaurant.

An irrational resentment irked me that she had not told me where she lived. She had kissed my cheek when we reached the street corner near Mme Duflot's establishment. It wasn't just a perfunctory pleasantry; it seemed to have some affection behind it, but it was brief. Did it demonstrate too much practice?

She had laughed in that disconcerting way she had when I'd pressed for her address, or at least a time for another *rendez-vous*.

"Don't worry, Charles," she had said. "We'll see each other again. This is Paris, and I think we go to many of the same places."

I stared into the fire and reflected how nearly a perfect evening it had been, but I remained dissatisfied. I was annoyed with myself for being so priggish and provincial, and for wanting that schoolboy knowledge of everything at once. No mysteries; as if a person's life, experiences and character could be gleaned over dinner. Yet, I felt there was a key to understanding her situation; one that could unlock the door and reveal an order to all the contradictions I saw.

I confess to priding myself for an ability to read people. Those I could trust; those I could not; who was bluffing, and who had real knowledge. I believed I was seldom wrong. This ability had served me well in business, and as an officer during the war. Once, when a popular officer disappeared with the regimental funds, it had not surprised me. In fact, I had a pretty good idea where the bounder had gone and had been right. However, by the time it was discovered, most of those involved were dead, and I took no pleasure in the outcome.

Natasha, I found harder to fathom, which perversely made her more attractive. Her contradictions were perplexing, and she did not give much away, though she didn't stop me from questioning her. As I said, I didn't know whether my attraction was to her or to her mystery; to the fact that she had been immortalised by several leading artists; or to the simpler fact that she was utterly unlike anyone I'd met before.

She was certainly totally unlike Danielle. Danielle was the daughter of one of the partners at Moreau, Doré et Cie. Not long after joining the company, which was very small, I grew aware of an expectation, or at least a hope, that I would find Danielle Doré of interest.

She was a typical French girl of the rising *bourgeoisie* who fully understood her place in the world. She was not unattractive but did nothing to make the most of her assets. She worked near me in the office (by accident or contrivance?) and was a pleasant colleague. Technically, she was senior to me, but she did not assert it. As any new employee would have been, I suspected that any misdemeanour would be reported by her.

Danielle was suitably distant, but one day, we met by accident at a nearby café where I sometimes went for lunch, and we ate together. Like so many girls of the period, the man she hoped to marry was killed in the war, and she continued to carry the gloom.

"Some of us get over it by drinking too much or having a succession of meaningless affairs," she said. "Others, like me, don't really want to forget and have families who will look after them – forever, if necessary. For us, love for anyone else will always be in the shadow of our first loves. No one will ever live up to the grand illusion of our memories."

I recognised Danielle's attitude and appreciated the candid warning. However, there were continuing subtle – and not so subtle – hints about the office that I should take advantage of a situation that could yield a good wife and a secure and profitable future. Danielle and I were given theatre or opera tickets, invited to parties, or sent to visit customers together.

We went, and for the most part, had a good time, but there was no magic. Sometimes I would feel guilty, but the pragmatic Danielle said that as long as I didn't hate being with her, to accept the tickets and enjoy the events. From time to time, she'd make an effort to wear her hair differently, or try different make-up. At the end of these evenings, when everyone was thinking that love was blossoming, Danielle would give me a light kiss at her doorstep and say, "Thank you, for understanding."

While we could be seen together several times a month, I was careful not to put myself in a position where the fiction took on a life of its own, and I ended up on the road to the altar. Still, our lack of expectations of each other made us more or less easy companions, and our trust, if not our affection, grew.

The perception of others meant that any real quest for love had to be more circumspect as I had to avoid being seen by those who were expecting me to marry Mlle Doré. Should I ever find a girlfriend, explaining the relationship with Danielle would require care lest she jumped to false conclusions. For her part, Danielle encouraged me to find true love, and repeatedly claimed to have told her parents that I was a friend and colleague, but nothing more. At present, neither of us had anyone so continued to live the myth.

I already thought that Natasha was as unobtainable as Danielle and saw little harm in planning to further our acquaintance until it reached its inevitable conclusion. Comfortable company was all that many could handle after so much tragedy and so many unfulfilled dreams.

Weary, and the fire dying, I went to bed and eventually fell into a restless sleep.

ൢ

Concentrating the next day was, not surprisingly, difficult. I was gnawing on the conundrum that was Natasha, and lack of sleep compounded my distraction. Shortly before lunch, Danielle came to my desk and sat in the bent wood chair next to it. She had a folder with variously sized papers in it. Order forms, invoices, cheques and other forms that enabled Moreau, Doré et Cie to function.

"Something's bothering you today, Charles," she said softly, passing a blank order form to me.

She was very good at this, but I always feared I'd do something to disclose the ruse.

"I was out late last night, and didn't sleep well," he said, pretending to check the order against my ledger.

"Was she pretty?" Danielle asked.

"I think she could be," I said, initialling the form and handing it back to her.

"Can you meet me at the café at lunchtime?" she asked, putting the paper back in her folder.

"I think that will be fine," I said, as she stood to go back to her desk.

I liked Danielle's sense of irony and self-parody. Once she had made her position clear, it was almost easy to relax with her, though I could never forget she was the boss's daughter.

The café was dingy, and the food mediocre at best, but it was convenient to the office and in warmer, drier, weather the outside tables were pleasant.

I told Danielle about meeting Natasha. She asked

some questions about the exhibition, and what sort of people were there, but she appeared to share my sense of intrigue and curiosity about the Russian girl. On the other hand, her laughter at the revelation about Natasha playing the piano at Mme Duflot's revived my embarrassment for being priggish.

"When are you seeing her again?" Danielle asked eagerly. "I'd like to meet her. Does she really call herself Madame X?"

The spontaneity of her barrage of questions made me laugh.

"It was just a chance encounter," I protested. "I doubt I'll ever see her again. I wouldn't know how to find her."

"You'll just have to go to Mme Duflot's," she teased. "Anyway, you just said that she expected you to encounter each other again."

"I doubt she meant it," I said, realising that I felt sad about that.

"Did you spend the whole evening calling her Madame X?" Danielle asked.

I explained about calling her Natasha, and how I suspected it wasn't her real name at all. I also shared that I had puzzled half the night as I tried to work out a plausible story for her.

"That's a really good problem," she said. "I'd like to work on that puzzle, too. It's a lot more interesting than ground millet. I think the thing to do is for you to take me along, so I can meet her."

I looked at her with disbelief.

"To Mme Duflot's?"

"No, you fool," she laughed. "She's bound to turn up at other galleries. She told you who she was posing for, now find out where they're selling their things."

For established artists, this would be possible, but for the young, starving ones, it would be more difficult. However, I had had the impression that Natasha didn't pose for nothing, and based on that, we might be able to track her down.

IV
Seeking Natasha

MY routine varied little over the next few weeks, except I was spending more time with Danielle. That had not been a deliberate development; she just joined me for lunches, coffees and dinners.

"You want to make your meeting with her look like chance, " Danielle said over a drink after work. "You don't want to give her the wrong impression; it should look accidental."

"So, you don't want me to lurk outside Mme Duflot's?" I teased.

"Well, it's up to you, but Madame X might get the wrong idea. I wonder why she's 'Madame' X, and not Mademoiselle X," Danielle mused. "Do you think she's married?"

"It sounded like she had no one," I said.

"Perhaps she's a widow," she speculated. "Let's see; her husband was a Grand Duke who was murdered in the revolution. She escapes and comes here penniless.

"Of course, it might be something more mundane," she added, sadly.

There was an amiable fug in the café that was in

marked contrast to the cold, wet evening. It was full of local people who either worked or lived in the area. There were nods, waves, and handshakes by nearly everyone who walked in. Danielle and I both knew that to be seen together after work would continue to fuel speculation in the office and the Doré family, but they were used to ignoring it whatever the source.

"Do you think we're boring?" Danielle asked.

"We? You and me?" I asked, surprised by the question. "Yes, I should say so."

"And does that not bother you?"

I remembered standing in the trenches, or patrolling an area on the same sort of night as this and aching for a boredom that was safe. If being inside a warm café, drinking with a young lady was boring, I'd choose it over the alternative.

Danielle sensed what I was thinking and began to apologise.

"No. Don't. My life *is* boring. Dull. Uninteresting. Predictable. And I am perfectly content."

Danielle nodded doubtfully.

"And you *are* still enjoying that?" she asked.

I nodded.

"Things are starting to happen, though," she said. "There are thousands of new people in Paris; from all over."

"If they don't want to buy grain powder, I don't care," I joked. "No, I'm not that far gone.

"You're right," I continued. "There are lots of new people and things going on. Much of it looks pretty ephemeral and probably is. Whether these are new contemporary values, or just colourful bandages to cover the wounds, I can't tell."

Danielle smiled at me.

"A lot of things will have to change," she said.

I looked at the table and the empty glasses.

"Do you want something to eat?" I asked.

"Yes, but not here."

We walked down the street to a small bistro around the corner. It was busy but we found a table and enjoyed the chatter of the other diners.

We reviewed the day's business while waiting for the order to be taken. Once the waiter had taken it and placed bread and wine on the table, Danielle returned to the subject of Natasha.

"Have you thought of how to find her without going to Mme Duflot's?" she asked.

I looked up sharply, surprised that this matter so occupied her.

"Well, what else are we going to talk about?" Danielle challenged. "Lorenz Frères's last order? Why Nicole is sulking, or if you think Etienne is smoking opium?"

She laughed.

"Come on, Charles, what else have we got to talk about?"

I shrugged. What she said was true enough, but not something I really wanted to face. Perhaps it was time I started to re-enter life; or at least, think about it. It was certainly time Danielle did.

"The best I can think of is to walk around to the gallery where I met her and see when their next show is; go to the opening and see if she's there."

Danielle was not impressed with my creativity, but couldn't think of anything better so remained silent, nibbling bread, until the first course arrived.

"Tomorrow's Friday," she began. "We can walk to the gallery after work and see if we can find out anything," she said. "Otherwise, it may have to be Mme Duflot's."

∽

That excursion, though a pleasant enough outing, yielded little. Galerie Hébrard was winding down the exhibition that I had attended, and most of the items had been sold. There would be no new show until late May, according to the young man.

Danielle was intrigued by the bust of Madame X, and spent much of the time in the gallery looking at it from different angles.

"How good a likeness is it?" she asked me.

"She looks like that when she's not speaking," I said. "Her face is lively when she talks. This makes her look more severe than she is."

Danielle continued to look at the exhibition while I went to speak to an assistant.

"Do you know the model for that piece?" I asked, nodding towards Madame X.

"I've seen her here at openings," he said. "She's one of those Russians with little to do. She's modelled for several sculptors and painters."

"You don't know anything more about her?" I prompted.

It was at this point that the assistant's looked changed to man-of-the-world mode and looked again towards Danielle.

Judging that records might be set for leaps to erroneous conclusions, I felt compelled to offer an explanation.

"I met her here at the opening, and we spoke," I began. "My wife thought she sounded interesting and said she'd like to see the piece and perhaps meet the model, too."

These lies flowed so easily that it frightened me, but I did not hesitate, redden, or avert my gaze from the young man.

"I'm sorry, monsieur," he began, but I raised a superior hand to stop him.

"I expressed my questions badly," I said, with authority.

He noted the date of the next opening in his agenda, and recorded my name for the invitation. Well, not just my name, but M. et Mme Charles Boivet.

On our way out, the young man said, "*Bonsoir, Mme Boivet,*" which prompted a sharp series of questions ten paces down the road. I endeavoured to explain but got the impression that she hadn't really been bothered.

For no reason, we turned down the Rue Saint Honoré, and found ourselves reading a menu on the window of a small bistro. Without bothering to ask, Danielle walked to the door and waited for me to open it.

ↄ⟨

Our lives ground on; work was steady, and the atmosphere was more confident. Danielle and I continued to have lunch together several times a week and perhaps a drink after work, but we hadn't done anything remarkable until Danielle suggested that we go to the theatre one evening.

"To be honest, Father gave me the tickets," she said, with her characteristic smile of acceptance. "M.Rosen gave him two tickets. It's being conducted by some Russian, and he's heard us talking about a certain Russian."

She smiled.

"It might be fun," she encouraged.

"I think it would," I replied, then looked at Danielle carefully. "You're thinking what I'm thinking, aren't you?"

She laughed.

"You're getting to know me."

ɞ

The concert was at Salle Gaveau in the VIIIth Arrondissment, about two miles from Moreau, Doré & Cie. It was a Friday evening, Danielle and I were both tired, and tempted to go for a drink, forget the concert and go home.

"No," I said, resolutely. "We must start making the effort."

We arrived at the hall with about ten minutes to spare and made our way up to the first balcony. The seats were on an aisle, about halfway up the right-hand side.

The auditorium was nearly full but with a noticeably wide variety of people. Some in pre-war evening dress; others, like us, dressed for a business day; while others were a motley. Danielle scanned the audience with her opera glasses, while I read the programme.

From a glance, I could see that all the music was Russian and that explained the variety of attire in the audience: the wealthy Russians were in the orchestra stalls, while the impoverished, who probably saved their centimes for the evening, were in the second balcony.

I was just reading about the conductor when thunderous applause made me look up. The conductor had just barely appeared from the wings, but he was obviously well-known and loved by this audience.

Some of the music I had heard: the spritely overture to *Ruslan and Ludmilla*, the theatrical *A Night on Bald Mountain*, and Tchaikovsky's melodic *Variations on a Rococo Theme*. Danielle, too, knew some of them, but the other Mussorgsky pieces and the ones by Liadow, and Scriabin, were unknown to both of us. And, while the short Glazunov arrangement of *Ey-Ouchnem* caused us to smile at each other, we saw that many in the crowd had tears on their cheeks. The piece was encored after tumultuous cheering and applause.

During the interval, Danielle spoke excitedly.

"There's something going on here," she said. "It's exciting! I feel like I am a guest at a private party and I don't know any of the other people, but they all seem to know each other and are passionate about them."

I wouldn't have expressed it that way but knew what she meant. Here was a body of people – maybe only a quarter of the whole audience – who had come together to share – to share what? Their music? Their admiration of this conductor? Their culture? Their past? Their lost dreams?

"Come!" Danielle said, pulling me up the steps to the aisle. "Let's go to the box office and get tickets for the next concert."

We wove and pushed our way through the throng and down the stairs.

"Wait here," I said to Danielle, as I waded through knots of people, many speaking in accented French or Russian, to the box office window.

I was queuing up and reading the poster with the different programmes when someone at my side spoke.

"Skip the next one, but go to the one on May sixth."

I turned to see Natasha.

She was dressed nearly as she had been when I'd first met her. She had a little more colour but still looked undernourished.

"I wondered if I might see you here," I said, smiling at her.

She returned a cautious smile.

"There are many people I know here. I have come with a lady who sometimes gives me piano lessons. I can't introduce you as she is surrounded by people who I don't want to see me."

We spoke briefly about the concert, and the next ones, and Natasha told me that I couldn't imagine the high regard in which Koussevitzky was held in Russia.

"Can I buy you a ticket for the sixth?" I asked, as I moved closer to the *guichet*.

"It would not be convenient," she said.

I understood that she didn't want me to buy her one, but didn't know why. I chose tickets in about the same place we were sitting tonight and was about to ask

Natasha to come to meet Danielle, but when I turned, she had gone.

Danielle was intrigued by the encounter, and amused that I had so readily taken her advice about which concert to choose.

"It makes no difference to me," she said. "Are women always able to get you to do what they want this easily?"

I laughed, but did not explain that I had learned that if little things make people happy, there was no reason not to do them, especially if they were of little matter to me.

"She said that the main work was Rachmaninoff's *Isle of the Dead*, and that she understood I was trying to get off it."

"Witty girl," Danielle said. "Witty and perceptive."

V
New Resolutions

It was nearly a week before I had the chance to speak to Danielle about the evening. We had been particularly busy: M. Moreau was travelling with one of his clerks, and the office was short-staffed. When we were able to meet late Friday afternoon, we agreed to go for a drink after work.

"Most of the office seems to think that we've fallen out," she said, as we were served our drinks under the café's awning.

"They must have something to talk about," I replied.

"All weekend, after the concert, I thought about the joy on the faces of all those Russians who had lost everything; just imagine if the Germans had won, and we had to flee to Spain, Norway or England. Could we ever be really happy again?" she asked.

There was real pain on her face.

"And, Natasha – you said she seemed afraid of seeing some people."

"She was afraid of being seen by them," I corrected.

"Can you imagine living like that? Who is she – or was she – that she should be so afraid?" she asked, with confusion and bewilderment in her eyes. "That all made me consider my life, and how I've been acting. I concluded that even if I'm unhappy, I don't have to be miserable. There's a lot happening right here in Paris; it's bright, loud, colourful, exuberant, possibly wrong-headed, but there does seem to be an excitement."

I nodded. These were common enough thoughts of people faced with what was rapidly transforming from the world of the last days of *la belle époque* of our childhood to whatever the noise and speed were bringing.

"We still need to be responsible; get on with business, meet our obligations, and ensure our work gets done, but we can enjoy things, too," Danielle continued. "There's no requirement to like everything we see or hear."

I waited before answering.

The café was full and noisy. The thick smoke pulsed in the room each time someone opened the door. Each person with his own history and world of problems. Yet, they were here, making conversation, drinking their beer or wine, laughing with friends, and enjoying a cigarette.

"We are both still climbing out of our trenches," I said eventually. "It takes time."

"Shall we help each other get out?"

Danielle had never been so forthcoming or personal.

"Can we? How?" I asked, but not negatively. "We can barely help ourselves."

Danielle looked like she was preparing herself for a high-dive. She looked down, took a few deep breaths, then returned her gaze to me.

"I don't think either of us is fit for a serious romantic encounter yet," she ventured.

She waited, as if expecting to be sharply contradicted, but I waited for her to continue.

"The hurt has been too great to have healed yet, but it will," she said, softly. "We can help prepare each other to re-join normal life."

These weren't things that could be made to happen, or planned. How false and artificial it would be; nature had to take its course. I began to protest.

"No, Charles," she said, gently. "My girlfriends are giving up on me and moving on. What you and I have been living is not normal life. We've just got used to it."

I knew the truth of this, but remained reluctant to admit it. While Danielle and I had shared time together, we had not shared intimacies. She knew nothing of my war experiences, and she had shared nothing about her fiancé, the circumstances of his death; how she had learned of it, or how she had coped in the early days of grief. The fact that she was my employer's daughter didn't help, but next to the other barriers, it was a negligible impediment.

"What do you suggest?"

She knew I'd ask, and she knew the answer, but

saying it was harder. She had intimated some of her thoughts before we went to the concert.

I was sympathetic to these efforts. Danielle was kind, hardworking and intelligent; at the same time, I could see something tragic in her I wished I could relieve.

"Are you willing to change?" she asked gently. "Are you willing to get out of your shell and take some risks again?"

She was getting uncomfortably close, and it made me feel claustrophobic. The feeling brought back memories of cowering in the trenches when the mortar shells were pummelling our position. Noise that didn't stop for hours on end, and felt that if it got any louder I would be deaf forever. As it was, when it stopped, my ears would ring for days, making any sort of communication with others a tiresome chore at a time when I only wanted to curl up and sleep.

I still couldn't think about that horror for more than a few seconds; the other things that came with the aftermath were harder to face, and they were the stuff of unbidden nightmares.

How could you explain that to anyone, especially someone who had lost a loved one in the carnage? No doubt Danielle's image of her fiancé's death was one that was clean and heroic, not the spattered mess that most were. There was no way I could talk about such things to anyone who hadn't been there.

"Charles?"

I heard Danielle's voice gently prompting.

"Are you all right?" she asked.

I looked up at her.

"You look pale!" she exclaimed, putting her hand to my cheek.

I wanted to shake her off and push her away but retained enough sense to know that she cared and was probably one of my closest friends.

"I'm sorry."

I took a breath, straightened up and faced her.

"You are right, of course," I said. "We both have more to offer the world than our current drudgery."

I stopped to find the courage to continue. Then, I laughed. I couldn't help it. To Danielle it must have seemed almost maniacal. She flinched and heads turned. I stood and went outside, leaving my coat on the chair.

Danielle instantly abandoned her drink, gathered my coat and followed me out.

She found me standing on the pavement by a tree, trying to light a cigarette. She said nothing, but put the coat around my shoulders, and stood close, looking into my face. She waited as I took a second long drag, then turned to blow the smoke away from her.

"I was trying to find the courage to answer you," I said.

"I once had the courage to run with a friend to rescue another soldier, and now I don't have the nerve to talk to you, sitting safely in a café."

Danielle said nothing, but stepped closer and put her arms around me and rested her head on my chest.

She began to speak, but I raised my hand and stroked her hair, and she remained quiet.

"You are right, of course," I said. "Right in your diagnosis, and probably right in your proposed cure.

"It is a new life we each must find," I managed to say. "We've been clinging to our old lives and trying to reclaim them. That won't work."

I flicked the cigarette into the gutter and gently put my arm around her shoulders and led her slowly towards her house. From where we were, it was the opposite direction to my own rooms. After walking a few hundred feet, Danielle stopped.

"I'll be all right, you go back. Get some rest," she said, separating herself from me. "I'm sorry. I shouldn't have – "

"No, Danielle. I'm glad you did. I've been acting like a cripple. It's time to recover."

She didn't reply but reached out and squeezed my hand.

"Shall we begin tomorrow?" I ventured.

She gave a big smile.

"I'll meet you here at ten. Let's each have two ideas of

things to do."

I laughed as I walked home. How quickly things could feel differently. To actually look forward to the next day was a novelty in itself.

℞

Later, Danielle told me that she, too, recognised feelings she hadn't known for more than five years: Optimism. Confidence. Anticipation.

She was absorbed with these sensations as she strode confidently towards her home. The boulevard unwound before her, bright, fresh, new, and filled with possibilities. She slowed her pace and looked in windows brightly illuminated. Fashions with bright colours and bold patterns; furniture with straight lines, shiny chrome and rich wood and leather; books piled high by not only French writers but English, German, Spanish, American and Russian, and magazines filled with photographs: people, cars, ships, glamorous hotels, beaches and art.

She had a lot of catching up to do, and on impulse went in and picked up various journals: *Mode du Jour, La Vie Parisienne, Vogue*. She flipped through each quickly, evaluating the pictures and copy. She felt above *Mode du Jour*'s price of twenty-five centimes, and was intimidated by *Vogue* and its four franc cost. However, impulse and vanity triumphed. She instantly knew that this was not a publication she could let her parents see both for the narcissism and cost, so she took her purchase into the café near her home to read it before sneaking it into her bedroom.

While there were many familiar faces in the café, none was more than an acquaintance, and no one would care what she was reading or what she'd paid for it.

Danielle found a table by the window, ordered a glass of the *cuvée de patron* and slipped the magazine out of the thin paper bag and began reading the table of contents.

The contrast between what she saw on the pages, and her own clothes, shoes, jewellery – in fact, her life – increased the realisation of her detachment.

She was reading an article about the textures of silk fabrics and the way they were dyed when she sensed someone near her.

"Good evening, Danielle," said a voice next to her. "Is this a rare or customary extravagance?"

She looked up expecting to see an old friend, but she saw a young lady whom she did not know take the seat opposite at her small marble-topped table.

The combination of guilt and surprise rendered her speechless as she gaped at the woman.

"I'm sorry," the young lady said, smiling. "I didn't mean to alarm you. I'd like to think that I am a friend of Charles. You may call me Natasha."

VI

In which Natasha reveals. . . very little

The waiter placed Danielle's wine on the table, and she asked for another glass for Natasha. Not asking her surprise visitor what she wanted put her in control, she thought, though in reality, she was still completely taken aback by the woman's presence and the realisation of how young she was.

Even if Natasha had not given her name, Charles's description of her was accurate enough to instantly identify her. Most noticeable to Danielle was the contrast between Natasha's dress and her deportment. She conducted herself like an aristocrat. Charles had alluded to this, but not expressed it as baldly, though, knowing Charles, perhaps he hadn't fully appreciated the level of her refinement, Danielle thought.

While she began speaking to Natasha, she took in as much as she could.

"Would you like something to eat?" she offered.

The girl's thinness, though part of her beauty, bordered on the distressing, and Danielle couldn't ignore it.

"Maybe later," Natasha replied.

They silently waited for her wine to arrive and studied

each other's features without apology. Natasha was used to being stared at, but Danielle felt her flesh crawl under the gaze of this stranger.

While Natasha looked poor, she was very clean. Her hair, fingers, nails, and even her unfashionable, thread-bare clothes were clean and cared for. She wore a hardly-noticeable touch of colour on her lips and cheeks. Not unexpectedly, there was no jewellery apart from a simple black bangle.

When Danielle returned her focus to Natasha, she was surprised to hear her saying:

"You are more attractive than you know," Natasha said, once the glass of wine was before her. "You have been in mourning for too long."

"What do you know of it?" Danielle asked, still on the defensive.

"Only what I see," Natasha replied. "Paris is full of injured souls. If it is not a good place for healing, it is a place where one can be distracted."

"And, are you an injured soul, too?"

Natasha gave the hint of a smile, and the tiniest tilt of her head before dropping her gaze to the hand that held her glass.

"I, too, must move on," she said. "Who is to say whose loss is worse? The girl who lost a lover, or the one who lost her country?"

Unable to find a reply, Danielle raised her glass.

"To healing," she said.

Natasha nodded and drank.

Natasha's accent was just as Charles had described. She had known other Russians through the business, but this accent was somehow different.

"Charles has told me all he knows about you," Danielle said. "It's not much, but he was taken with you and would like to know you better."

"And, would you let him?" Natasha asked.

Danielle looked down. The question hurt more than it should have, and she was less sure of the answer than she had been earlier in the evening.

Natasha reached forward and rested her hand on Danielle's.

"I see you would," she said, and Danielle immediately looked up at her.

She was surprised to find Natasha smiling at her.

"That is the best way to keep him," she said, gently. "But, let me reassure you that I have no designs on him. Apart from that, it wouldn't be safe for me – or Charles."

Natasha squeezed Danielle's hand with sympathy. Danielle watched the long, thin fingers gently curve over the back of her hand, and sensed their strength.

"Charles said you play the piano," she said.

"My concert venue isn't particularly respectable, so I

55

doubt you'll hear me play," she said, releasing her affectionate hold.

Danielle laughed which surprised Natasha.

"Charles told me that, too."

"I am surprised."

"It was an interesting part of your story," she said. "But what makes you talk about your safety – and Charles's? Are you in some danger?"

"Not if I am careful," Natasha said.

"There are lots of Russians in Paris; you must have many friends."

Natasha looked away for a moment, then said, "I do not wish to speak of such things. Not all of your countrymen are your friends."

Danielle couldn't separate what Natasha had said from how she said it. It wasn't the accent which had been carefully taught and learnt, it was also her choice of words and grammar that was distinctive. While there was the Russian bluntness, odd curious word choices or an old fashion phrase, Danielle knew that education had figured dominantly in her earlier life.

Not dissuaded by Natasha's answer, Danielle pressed on:

"Charles would like to do something for you."

Natasha looked wary.

"I am not a war charity," she said, but not unkindly.

"What would he do?"

"He said you looked like you weren't eating well," she said tentatively, then she laughed, and her manner relaxed. "I think men come to conclusions, and he is still vulnerable."

Natasha looked at Danielle with curiosity. The laugh had surprised her.

"How is my hunger related to Charles's vulnerability?" she asked.

Hearing Natasha refer to Charles so familiarly caught her off guard and she could not instantly reply.

"I – I meant only that Charles is sensitive; he wants to help people, but sometimes feels powerless to do so."

"He bought me dinner," Natasha replied, looking directly at Danielle.

Danielle recaptured her own efficient manner.

"He – and I – would like to do something to help your life in a more lasting way," she said, but was uncertain exactly what she meant. "Charles had the feeling that your life was – precarious."

Natasha drank her wine and smiled.

"I have lived through my precarious life," she said. "It is remarkably stable now. I have the work with costumes; I have Madame Duflot's; I have some modelling. At the moment, I'm actually quite comfortable. M. Du Beaumont is not a good painter, but he is friends with Picasso and Duchamp and if one of them paints me, others will follow."

"And that's not precarious?"

Natasha looked suddenly tired. Her body seemed to shrink and fade as Danielle watched her gulp the last of her wine, and observed how carefully and properly she held her glass.

"M. Du Beaumont has a comfortable house," she said quietly. "It's better than sleeping under snow-covered haystacks."

She then recovered herself, stood, straightened her coat and extended her hand in an almost regal manner.

"Thank you, Mlle Doré," she said. "I hope I will see you and Charles soon. Keep close to him; you don't want to let him go."

Again, Danielle was taken aback but recovered quickly enough to speak before Natasha vanished.

"I am meeting Charles tomorrow," she said using her business voice. "Ten o'clock at the *Café L'Homme d'Affaires.* Please come."

Natasha locked eyes with her, but gave no hint of a reply before turning and walking into the evening.

VII

Ouvre tes yeux!

When I arrived at the café shortly before ten on Saturday morning, I was shocked to see Natasha sitting at a table in the sun, drinking a *café noir*. I looked around for Danielle before saying good morning.

Natasha looked up from a newspaper and smiled at me.

"I may be pale, but I am not a ghost," she said, laughing.

I looked about again and sat down.

"Don't look so worried," she said. "Danielle told me to meet you here."

A waiter stopped, and I ordered a *café au lait*.

"You've spoken to Danielle?" I asked, feeling that I had lost all touch with what was going on.

"We are going to improve our lives," she said without a hint of irony. "It's what we all need, and you and Danielle most."

Questions raced through my mind, mostly to do with what she and Danielle had been talking about. I also wanted to know what she had been doing since we'd had our meal; whether she was healthy; if she had enough to eat; who she was modelling for, and where she was living, but was unable to ask a single one.

"How do you know Danielle?" I managed to ask. "You disappeared before I could introduce you at the concert."

"I saw her with you, of course," she replied. "Sitting proudly in the first balcony watching over the rest of us with her spy-glasses."

"Isn't that unfair?"

"What's fair in this world?" Natasha asked distractedly, but then turned to me. "No. You are right. When I spoke to her, she was very kind."

"Where did you see her?"

"In a café," she replied without expression. "We had a glass of wine and a chat about fashion."

I must have looked sceptical.

"I can *talk* about fashion, can't I?" Natasha asked bluntly.

I laughed and shook my head.

"I wasn't surprised about *you* talking about fashion," I said, still laughing. "I was amused by the idea of Danielle talking about it."

Natasha smiled.

"Oh, Charles, you must be careful," she said softly and reached for my hand.

"Careful of what?"

I never got an answer. Natasha looked up and smiled,

and when I looked around, Danielle was approaching the table. I stood and drew out a chair for her, as Natasha extended her hand. For an instant, Danielle looked confused as to what to do with Natasha's hand, but she took it and gave it a gentle squeeze before releasing it.

By the time Danielle had settled, the waiter had come over and I ordered coffee and some brioches. Danielle recognised this as an attempt to feed Natasha but was also certain that Natasha had recognised the ruse.

"Are you still playing the piano?" Danielle asked, giving me a mischievous glance.

"Yes, and in the same place," she said. "I know you think it is inconvenient, but it's the best I can do."

"And modelling?"

"Jacques Du Beaumont," she said. "He's not a particularly good painter, but his apartment is dry, most of the time."

"Is he the only one you're modelling for?"

"It takes time to finish a picture, and I don't change lovers that often. I have a pre-war face that only certain artists like," she said.

She had continued her answer so smoothly that I hardly registered what she had said until a few moments later, by which time, the conversation had moved on. It was only on reflection that I realised that this had been a carefully executed exchange for my benefit. Danielle hadn't reacted at all to the news that Natasha was living with the painter, or talking openly about playing at Mme Duflot's. That had surprised me most until I figured it out.

"There are lots of younger girls, too," Natasha continued, then sighed. "No one as good as Amadeo will paint me again."

"Modigliani painted you?" Danielle asked in surprise. "I don't know much, but even bourgeois families like mine have heard of him."

I laughed to myself at Danielle's characteristic frankness.

"It wasn't a particularly good painting," Natasha said. "I think Jeanne was jealous of me, and Madeo was afraid to make me look too attractive."

The coffee and brioches came and I left the basket in front of Natasha until she took one.

"Where's the painting now?" Danielle asked.

She shrugged.

"It wasn't sold when I left the studio. That was only a few months before he died," she said. "Who knows where all his things went. Jeanne killed herself the next day, and I suppose quite a bit of it was stolen – probably by the landlord who hadn't been paid. He probably passed them on to other creditors."

She shrugged again.

"It might turn up one day."

I noticed that although I had not seen Natasha eat a piece of her brioche, it was gone.

We drank our coffee and watched the crowds in amiable silence.

"If you like new paintings, I can show you some that are apt to be good ones," Natasha said. "There's a gallery with new artists. Come!"

She stood and moved away from the table to the pavement. I put a handful of coins in the coaster, and quickly followed Danielle, who had been as fast on her feet as Natasha.

We turned down to the Rue de Rivoli toward Place de la Concorde. After pausing to admire the space, the obelisk and the Hôtel de Crillon, we promenaded up Avenue Gabriel, pausing again to look at the *Palais de l'Élysée*. Natasha turned up Avenue Victor Emmanuel III to Rue la Boëtie.

She stopped at windows that displayed large, colourful canvases with extraordinary shapes and figures.

"I could just about handle Modigliani," Danielle whispered to me, taking my hand. Later that day, I reflected on that gesture and recognised it as a small indication of possession; but whether it was for me to recognise, or for Natasha, I could not be sure.

I gave a small laugh, not wanting to be rude to Natasha, who boldly pushed the door to the gallery open and strode in.

"Ouvre tes yeux!" she said loudly and everyone in the room turned.

A slim, neat-looking man with a moustache approached, and Danielle and I anticipated being ejected. As he grew closer, the expression on his face transformed into a broad grin, and he took Natasha's hand and kissed it.

"You have come to see our latest pieces?" he asked.

"I have come to show them to friends," she said.

He greeted us with a level of formality impeccably pitched between Natasha's Bohemian affectation and our bourgeois expectations. One never knew who had money. Or taste. He invited us to take our time, and to ask him any questions we might have. Natasha was already in a corner looking closely at a painting, moving closer, then backing away and becoming lost in it.

I led Danielle to the opposite corner where we began making our way through the collection. There were names we recognised but knew little about: Renoir, Cezanne, Duchamps, Picasso, Braque, and others we had not encountered: Soutine, Rouault, Léger.

Danielle was far more comfortable in these surroundings than I, so I remained quiet, aware that I knew nothing about what I was seeing, even though I instinctively reacted positively towards most of it.

When we felt we had seen everything, we looked around for Natasha. We found her engaged in a lively conversation with a man in his early thirties. Tanned, athletic looking, they seemed to be friends.

As we walked to her, we heard that they were speaking Russian. Natasha smiled at us and extended a hand to bring us closer.

"Charles and Danielle, this is Vladimir," she said with more assurance than either of us had seen. "Vladimir's family and mine were old friends in St Petersburg, yet we have both ended up in Paris."

"It was remarkable," Vladimir said. "We met at the Ballet Russes. We were both working with Natalia; Natasha with costumes and me on the sets. It wasn't until Natasha brought a hamper of costumes to the theatre that we met."

Both Vladimir and Natasha's accents had become much stronger as a result of their conversation in Russian, and Danielle and I could barely understand their French, let alone determine who they were talking about. We were pleased to see that Natasha had friends and wasn't always in hiding.

"When we are in rehearsal again, you must come see us all," he said expansively.

"I must go, Vladimir," Natasha said. "My friends will be wanting lunch."

She held out her hand to him, and he kissed it.

VIII
Present or Past?

There was a small restaurant on Avenue Victor Emmanuel III where we found a table. The weather had changed and looked threatening, so we went inside.

We hadn't spoken since leaving the gallery; Natasha because she looked like she wanted to make her feeling of happiness last as long as possible; Danielle and I because we were still taking in what we had seen.

We ordered from the simple menu, and wine and bread was quickly put on the table. I poured glasses for all of us.

"Thank you, Natasha," I said, raising my glass.

"You can always go there and look," she said. "Sometimes the artists are there, and sometimes you meet old friends."

"You really knew Vladimir in St Petersburg?" Danielle asked, adding, "as children," lest Natasha thought she had made it up.

"Yes; my father knew Vladimir's parents. His father was the late Tsarina's banker," she said, crossing herself in the Orthodox style. "They lived near us. Father knew him from business.

"It was strange to meet him again here in Paris," she continued. "I'd been in Paris longer; he came immediately after the first Revolution; most people knew that Kerensky wasn't strong enough to withstand both the Bolsheviks and the remaining Tsarists."

"White Russians?" I asked.

"That's the common name, but there were Whites of every colour except Red," Natasha said. "That made them unreliable and weak. They only became unified after it was too late."

She fell silent and ate some bread.

I glanced at Danielle who returned the glance, again, surprised at the scope – and source – of her knowledge.

"Tell us what you thought of the paintings, and why," I said.

Natasha smiled and seemed to relax once more. She spoke about colour, spontaneity, seeing things afresh.

"Taking painting out of the studio was just the beginning," she said, enthusiastically. "There has now been time to build on the work of the Impressionists, but theirs was the first major break with stultified, ossified rules, and rigid, academic conventions. Oh, there is still an important place for schools to teach the skills and the craft, but what these new painters are showing is that you can't teach Art.

"My piano teacher says, 'You shouldn't be ruled by

technique,' but she *never* questions its importance."

The*ir* meal arrived, and the conversation became ✓ more general.

"You persuaded me to change our concert plans, so what do we have to look forward to?" I asked.

"More Russians, of course!" she laughed. "A piece by Liadow that I don't know; excerpts from *Petrushka* – which is quite tuneful – a Glazunov violin concerto that no one has heard, and Borovsky is playing Scriabin."

She announced this last item with such enthusiasm that Danielle asked:

"Another old friend of yours?"

She nodded.

"As a child, I heard him play in Russia. Later, I heard him here," she said. "He is an exceptional pianist, though you might find the Scriabin a bit strange. I can explain – "

She stopped suddenly, and her face froze. Danielle and I turned to see what had caught her eye. Two men were taking their seats towards the back of the restaurant.

"Don't look," she whispered sharply.

"What is it?"

"*Okhrana*," she whispered, then quietly slipped on her coat, and stood up. "I'll see you at the concert."

She left the restaurant unobtrusively and merged into the passing crowd.

Danielle and I stared at each other in total

bewilderment.

"*Ça alors! C'était quoi, ça?*" Danielle asked, still looking confused.

We turn around to look at the ordinary-looking men talking to the waiter.

"Well, that's one way to get out of paying for lunch," I said, but Danielle didn't laugh.

"Do you think she's in trouble?" she asked. "She's clearly frightened."

I had no reply.

"She was just beginning to open up," she continued. "I had the feeling that if we could keep her talking, we might learn something about her."

I shook my head.

"She's never going to open up. She's been Madame X too long to risk it."

We sat quietly as the waiter cleared the dishes. I ordered a coffee; Danielle still had nearly a full glass of wine.

"If she was frightened of them – "

"She's Russian, Danielle. You'll never figure her out," I said. "Now, tell me what you really thought of the paintings."

෨

We returned via the Metro from Marbeuf to Tuileries where we went into the gardens for a drink. We had kept off the subject of Natasha all the way from the restaurant, but Danielle's curiosity got the best of her.

"What was it that she said when she saw those men?"

"It sounded like 'okra'," I said.

Danielle nodded.

"It must be Russian. What can it mean?"

"I was serious, Danielle," I began. "I don't think it's a good idea to dig too deeply into Natasha's life."

Danielle looked amused.

"You don't approve of her sleeping with painters in exchange for a roof over her head?" she teased.

"I'm beyond judging people," I said. "Especially when we know nothing of her circumstances."

"Does that mean I shouldn't invite her for lunch with my parents?"

Danielle was taking pleasure in teasing me now. It was something she'd never tried doing before and the uncertainty of my response added to the fun.

"I think she'd be charming company, and secretly grateful for a good meal, but they'd have to get that old Pleyel tuned," I replied without a flicker of irony or irritation.

She looked at me to see if I were serious. Only then did I break into a broad smile.

"It's her past that I think you should be careful about," I said. "And, if she is a fugitive, it's doubtful that she's causing any trouble now. If there are people from her past who wish her harm, then you and I are in no position to help her, other than with food, drink and company. Anyway, we barely know her – and it's likely to stay that way."

Danielle was keen to pursue this conversation, but the few touches of rain that we had felt on entering the gardens was rapidly turning into a soaking shower. We hurried to the Rue de Rivoli to catch bus or a tram to their homes.

As we parted, Danielle reached out and took my hand. I stopped and faced her and was met by her best smile.

"Thank you for a very interesting day!"

IX
Grey

The rain settled in and continued on and off for the next ten days. While warm temperatures brought the bushes and trees into leaf with the freshness that not even the Impressionists could capture, it kept us inside, and essentially on our own.

We reverted to our previous mode of living, meeting only on Fridays for a drink before going home. While no more was said about inviting Natasha to lunch, Danielle continued to nurture the plan.

As if in keeping with our plans, the weather cleared the day before the concert and the spirit of Paris lifted. We met at the Louvre Metro station. Danielle had gone home early to change, but not having her excuse of being the owner's daughter, I could not do likewise.

I confess to seldom noticing what Danielle wore, but this evening she wore a shorter dress than usual, with an embroidered oriental pattern. It had full sleeves, and some sort of cape about her shoulders. With it, she wore a velvet soft hat of the same green as the dress. The immediate effect was that she looked much younger, but even I knew it was probably not a good idea to say so.

"You have indulged yourself," I said. "No one will be watching the soloists."

At first, Danielle was uncertain of what I meant but appeared satisfied when I finished.

As at the previous concert, there were great crowds with the same mix of Parisians, and rich and poor Russians. I recognised some of them from before; many were wearing the same clothes. Their hair, beards, hats and caps made them instantly identifiable. Their exuberance on entering and taking their seats earned unsubtle glances of disdain from the nobler Russians, but the Parisians appeared to take it as a normal crowd for a Russian concert.

We looked for Natasha, but did not see her.

"Where was she sitting the last time?" Danielle asked.

"I didn't see her in the audience," he said. "She must be directly above us."

Koussevitzky took the stage with the same adulation as he had enjoyed at the previous concert. While he smiled and bowed, he didn't look completely comfortable.

While I was not particularly musical, Danielle had studied the piano through her school years and achieved a reasonable standard. She could play the easier Chopin works, but preferred Schubert, Schumann, Bizet and Saint-Saens.

While she hadn't said anything at the time, Danielle

resented my comment about "that old Pleyel." She was very fond of it, and it was, in fact, tuned annually.

The first half of the concert progressed quickly. *Petrushka* had been a lively contrast to *De l'Apocalypse*, though both had been received equally well.

We shuffled with the crowd down to the foyer and looked for Natasha. Danielle saw several people she knew from the business and exchanged greetings with them while I looked for Madame X without success.

The second half presented two surprises. A printed slip of paper in the programme announced that due to a misprint, the Glazunov concerto would be the familiar A Minor, not the *second* violin concerto as suggested by the advertisement. We had both heard the violin concerto before and were pleased to hear it again. *Prometheus* (*Poème de Feu*) was more difficult, with unfamiliar rhythms, chords, the large chorus and coloured lighting.

The Scriabin lasted only twenty minutes or so, but seemed much longer, though the audience reacted with its usual enthusiasm, cheering Borovsky loudly.

As they made their way down the stairs and through the foyer, we again scanned the crowd for Natasha without success. On the pavement, we continued to look about for her.

"Shall we wait?" Danielle asked, when she was unexpectedly taken by the arm.

"This way," Natasha said, leading us briskly around a corner, down an alley and into the next street.

When they slowed, we looked at her. She was dressed completely in grey with a shawl over her head. Had the evening been any darker, I would have believed we were being spirited away by a ghost.

"There's a café over there," she said, leading them across the road.

It was possibly the dingiest café in the Eighth Arrondissment, but Natasha seemed both familiar and comfortable with it. A handful of less affluent locals were dotted around. At two tables, men were playing cards, and a girl sat at a banquette against the wall staring at her small glass of wine. Its darkness was probably its main characteristic, and undetermined shapes of smoke hovered with a slight peristaltic action.

Natasha smiled and sat at a table several places from the nearest other patron.

"This will be fine," she said, as we sat down, trying not to look too puzzled.

"Another triumph, wasn't it?" she asked, enthusiastically. "To hear that music so far from home. You can't imagine the joy it brings. You could see it in the faces of my countrymen."

"They are very enthusiastic," I said.

"Can you imagine what it means to exiles to hear one

of their own leading an orchestra in a different country's capital and playing *their* music? It means the Russia they knew – *we* knew – continues to exist in our hearts and through the music we can share it. For us, it is like being back home for a while."

Danielle and I were silent for as Danielle had observed, we knew that situation could have been ours.

"We looked for you in the interval," Danielle said, coming from the reverie. "And we've been worried about you since the last time we saw you."

Natasha waved at the bar tender who seemed to be on this own; he eventually came to the table. She ordered bread and wine, when he went to fetch them, she continued.

"They have two or three dishes that are actually good. Their *andouillette*; and they usually have *coq au vin* or *boeuf bourguignon*, depending what day it is. The *bourguignon* is good, but it can taste more like goulash because the cook is Hungarian."

The wine came and Danielle and I ordered with some trepidation.

After eating two pieces of bread, Natasha picked up her wine glass.

"To friends, good music, and great art!" she exclaimed, laughing.

"So, what did you think of the concert," she asked

after draining half her glass.

"*Prometheus* was unusual," I said tentatively.

"Ah! Sasha is a nice man, but he thinks too much," she said. "Anatoly is good when controls himself. He's a quiet man, and his best music reflects that, like the piece tonight. And *Petrushka*? Did you not enjoy that?"

"I liked it a lot," Danielle said. "It has so much life."

"That's the difference between Prokofiev and Stravinsky," Natasha said. "Their music is equally full of life, but Stravinsky's isn't life as we know it, yet."

We all laughed, then I returned to Danielle's earlier comment.

"Are you all right, Natasha? Last time, when you left the restaurant so quickly, we were very concerned," I said.

"I'm fine," she said, dismissively. "When you come from a country that's recently had a revolution, it is inevitable that refugees meet up in foreign centres. Unfortunately, people who have lost their homeland bring their grievances and prejudices with them, even though in their new surroundings, they mean nothing."

"Are you being pursued?" I asked.

"I don't think many people know I exist," she said. "But, there are people whom I think it is safer not to meet."

The *boeuf bourguignon* goulash arrived with another basket of bread.

"How is M. Du Beaumont?" Danielle ventured.

"Don't talk to me about that pig!" she said, sharply. "It's a good thing he's a terrible painter otherwise I would feel more badly about leaving him."

"Where – " Danielle began to ask, but she caught my eye and I gave the slightest shake of my head and she stopped. "*Bon appetite*," she said instead.

Despite our misgivings, the food was good, and the wine better than expected.

Natasha chattered about a forthcoming performance of a Prokofiev work by the Ballet Russes. Danielle and I were getting better at keeping up with the names Natasha peppered her conversation with.

"He wrote it for Diaghilev a few years ago, but Diaghilev didn't like it. Stravinsky talked about doing it, but never did. Now, Prokofiev's made a lot of changes, but it's a very stupid story. If you liked the music from *Petrushka*, you might like this. Just sit there with your eyes closed," she said.

"What's it called?" Danielle asked.

Natasha laughed.

"It has a very long name in Russian that translates something like *The Fool Who Gets the Better of Seven Other Fools*. Diaghilev is calling it *Chout*."

As we ate, the conversation slowed and moved to more mundane subjects. I could tell that Danielle was still dying to ask Natasha where she was living, but I thought it best not to know. I doubted she'd tell us.

When we finished, I shared out the last of the wine and we sat back in our chairs.

"What are you doing over the summer, when the ballet is closed?" Danielle asked.

I smiled to myself as this was a clever way of getting an answer to the question she couldn't ask.

"Madame Duflot's never closes," she replied with a smile. "But I will be spending time in Gargenville where my piano teacher has a house. She invites students to come for a time each summer. Madame Duflot doesn't like it, but I tell her that without adequate instruction, her patrons won't like my music, and if they are not happy. . . ."

She laughed.

"Speaking of which, what time is it?"

When I told her, she grabbed her shawl and put it over her head and around her neck.

"I must not be late! Madame Duflot will be furious!" she exclaimed. "It was good to see you, my friends. Thank you for dinner."

As we watched her disappear out the door, the bill was brought to the table. All we could do was laugh.

"She's a clever lady."

"She's a survivor," Danielle said. "Besides, didn't you want to help her?"

X

Weddings

Several weeks passed, and Danielle and I saw nothing of Natasha. Work kept us occupied, and, indeed, had required long hours, after which all we wanted to do was retire to our own homes and beds.

We had the odd coffee or drink after work but had not dined together since the concert, nor had we spoken about Natasha.

The weather had warmed and the streets were noticeably busier, the cafés more crowded, and it seemed to take longer to get from A to B. The increased traffic brought with it an unwelcome amount of refuse in the streets: newspapers, cigar and cigarette butts, discarded wrappings, and fruit and vegetable pieces near market stalls and street vendors. The motor car had not yet fully taken over, and evidence of horses – even cows and sheep in certain areas – were still all too common encounters.

Yet, in early morning, when the street sweepers and cleaners were out, and the water washed the pavements and ran through the city's gutters, Paris regained the smell that people wanted to remember.

Unfortunately, by the time Danielle and I went for

our Friday evening drinks, conditions had deteriorated to an unappetising level, made worse by the heat of the day. Our route through Les Halles was particularly unpleasant, and we quickly made our way to the boulevard de Sébastopol and over Pont de Change.

We knew where we wanted to be: in the small bistro on the Quai d'Anjou on the Île Saint Louis.

The Angevin was on the leafy northeast corner of the island with outdoor seating that sometimes extended to the other side of the road. While we were not the only people in Paris with the same idea, we were able to find a table.

It was instantly cooler as we moved into the shade on the island, and once seated, a breeze coming off the water refreshed us.

We drank a light white wine with grilled fish and *frites* and gradually cast off the business week. I was growing used to being with Danielle and had missed our more frequent encounters, but whether that was just familiarity and habit or something more, I could not tell.

Danielle had not yet moved on; Henri was not yet buried in her mind, but she knew the time spent with me had helped. For now, our joint resolution to resurrect ourselves and the challenge of solving the "mystery of Madame X" enabled her to continue our chaste liaison.

We ate at a leisurely pace, enjoying the food, the

gradual cooling of the day, and unpressured conversation.

As the waiter cleared the dishes and we considered desserts, Danielle posed a question:

"Would you be willing to go to a ballet?"

"I can always close my eyes and enjoy the music," I said, not for the first time.

"Well, I'm not sure you'll be able to do that," she said. "It's a brand new one. M. Gauvin gave my father tickets. His son is playing clarinet in the orchestra. He says the music's pretty strange, but we haven't done anything since *Chout*."

"More Stravinsky?" I asked, though I had enjoyed the selections from *Petrushka*.

Danielle laughed.

"Not this time," she said. "Some home-grown renegades."

"Some?"

"Apparently, five composers put together this piece – it's called a ballet, but could be anything – with each of them writing a few sections. Cocteau wrote the story."

"He's no fool," I said. "Possibly crazy, but very clever. What's the piece?"

Danielle laughed again.

"It's called *Les Mariés de la Tour Eiffel*. The Ballets Suédois is doing it. Don't pretend you have anything else on that night. Who knows, we might see Natasha there."

"When?"

"Next Saturday. The eighteenth," she replied. "At the Théâtre des Champs Elysées."

"They are enjoying doing the revolutionary performances."

It had been nearly ten years since the riotous premiere of *Le Sacre du Printemps* at the same theatre, but the horrors of war had wiped the incident from the public, if not the artistic, memory. Yet, the descriptions of the evening had always made me regret that I had not been there.

Danielle said no more about the ballet. She wasn't certain whether I really wanted to go, but it fit with her plan.

We ate dessert in companionable silence and watched the traffic on the river. As the heat and humidity of the day diminished, we enjoyed the last of the wine and several cups of coffee.

∽

When the evening of the ballet came, I was less than excited by the whole excursion, even though we planned to have a good meal afterwards. Danielle accepted this reluctance, perhaps hoping that what promised to be an unconventional performance would cheer me up.

Once again, she had dressed in what I thought was a smart compromise of the latest modern fashion with a dress of a modest length, but with the shawl, beads and a few feathers to let it be known that she kept up with things.

"Don't you get a thrill from coming to something like this?" she asked. "Few people know what to expect. It's another of those mixed audiences with the old guard who feels the obligation to support the arts and be seen at events of note, and the near rabble of artists and *émigrés*."

I didn't reply. Nothing thrilled me. One day, I might regain my sensibilities and full awareness of my surroundings, but I was too used to blocking it out. I sometimes thought that a ravishing young woman could throw herself at me, and I'd merely raise an eyebrow at the curiousness of her actions and be otherwise unmoved.

Danielle wasn't throwing herself at me; I knew that, but the mutuality of effort that she sought was not yet manifesting itself.

I watched her as she climbed the stairs. With a bit more effort, she could be elegant, and probably very attractive, but if she didn't know, or know how, didn't care, or was not ready to do so, I didn't know.

What I did know, was that she was becoming a very shrewd business woman with great ability. I admired the way she negotiated purchases, sales and shipments. She kept track of everything; knew everyone's credit worthiness and tactics. Yet, her conversations, no matter how tough, were lubricated with questions about family, their own business conditions and plans, and amiable chit-chat.

However, Danielle was not a gossip. I had heard other women who worked in the company saying that they had confided in her about this or that and she had never betrayed them. Her friendly business conversations were to the point, and she did not waste time on the telephone, or in meetings.

As we made our way to our seats, Danielle waved to two or three people she knew. I knew no one.

Though I had visited the theatre often when on leave and since the end of the Great War, I had never been to the Théâtre des Champs Elysées and was used to the opulence of Paris's older theatres. The modernist architecture and sparseness of its design I found cold and soulless, but once in the auditorium, I liked the way that it directed my focus to the stage and did not offer mock-Baroque distractions.

"One day, we will say that we were at the opening night of *Le Mariés de la Tour Eiffel* and saw – " she glanced at her programme, "Milhaud, Poulenc, Auric, Honnegar, and Germaine Tailleferre. Do you know any of them?"

I nodded.

"I knew a chap in the army who worked for Poulenc's father's pharmaceuticals company," I said. "He said he might help me get a job with them after the war."

"Didn't it appeal?" Danielle asked.

"It did, very much, but Jean-Claude was killed two days later, and I never had the heart to see if I could work there."

"Their loss," Danielle said, and squeezed his arm. "I'm sorry to have brought up sad memories."

"He told me that M. Poulenc was against his son going into music," I said after a pause. "He's largely self-taught."

Danielle smiled.

"Then we could be in for anything."

The lights went down and the music began. The brightness of the set as the curtain went up almost hurt my eyes. Bright, primary colours on the flats and costumes created an instant atmosphere of celebration, and the music was, as Danielle had reported, lively, if a little strange.

Unlike other ballets I had seen – or more accurately, listened to, as I usually closed my eyes to enjoy the music and ignore the grotesque and repetitive acrobatics – this one, however, had a running commentary by two narrators (dressed as gramophones), and the music had been, as Danielle had said, "composed" by five different people.

While nonsensical things were happening on stage, sections of the audience were restless, and expressed disapproval with sniffing, coughing, shuffling, and the occasional outcry, but there was no violence or rioting as there had been with *Le Sacre du Printemps*.

On the whole, it was well received, as the exuberance of the company proved to be infectious, and the music was bright and tuneful compared to the more extreme cacophonies the audience had been experiencing elsewhere.

Danielle was uncharacteristically silent as we walked to the restaurant, presumably giving me a chance to consider what we had seen. Shortly before we arrived, I burst out laughing.

"What wonderful nonsense!" I exclaimed, loudly.

Danielle took my arm.

"I thought so, too!" she said, her face showing a carefree delight I had not seen before.

Over dinner, we discussed the postcard look of the sets; the stylised dancing, and the enthusiastic reception by the majority of the audience.

"I think there are some people there just to be watched," Danielle said. "I don't know about these things, but in those circumstances, it hardly seems to matter."

"It would be nice to know if it *meant* anything," I said, amused by this thought. "But perhaps, that's the point; especially after what the world has been through. Does *anything* really *mean* anything?"

I saw the shadow on Danielle's face.

Bitter memories were even now easily triggered and difficult to recover from. I had certainly not intended this sudden change in mood. It had been as accidental as her unknowing prodding of the bruise of Jean-Claude's death.

"I'm sorry," I said.

"Was there really no point?" she asked, barely audibly.

I felt I'd spoiled her evening, as she drank her coffee in silence.

XI

Summertime

Most of the following week passed before I had a chance to speak to Danielle about anything more than business. I sensed that she knew what I wanted to talk about and didn't seem ready to do so.

Eventually, I found her at *L'Homme d'Affaires* after work Thursday.

I greeted her when I sat down, but said nothing further until my glass of wine arrived. I was trying to judge her mood when she began.

"I think you were right," she said, hesitantly. "When you asked if there was really no point to it all. There was an obvious point: we retained our independence but at a terrible cost. In the process, we seem to have lost the way of life we were fighting for.

"On the other hand," she resumed after a pause, "what would be the point if things didn't change? Would it not inevitably lead to another war? All this noise, and experimentation must be to find a new – better – way of doing things."

These comments revealed Danielle's greater depth of perception than my own, and I was delighted to discover it. It was unusual for her to confide in me this way. These ideas had been thought about carefully and had caused her no little pain. I knew my response would need to be equally considered as my own future with her could turn on it.

"Some things must remain the same, too," I said. "People have to go to work, turn up on time, pay their bills, and buy food. The frivolity that we saw, was fun, but it wasn't life, and never will be."

Danielle seemed pleased with this reply, but didn't know how to show it. Smiling would have been wrong, but my thoughts appeared to coincide with her own, though from a wholly different experience. To demonstrate her feeling of understanding, she reached across the table and put her hand on mine.

I may have flinched in surprise, but she didn't notice as she had, too; it had been so long since she had touched anyone with affection.

I looked at her and gave a small smile, and put my other hand lightly over hers. I didn't look at her but at my hand on hers. Danielle made no attempt to move and it wasn't until a sudden breeze swept up the road, blowing dust and flapping awnings, that we disengaged and looked around.

With the wind came a sudden drop in temperature and a rumble of thunder.

"The rain won't be far behind," she said, looking about.

"Shall we find somewhere to eat?" I asked.

She nodded and we headed quickly toward Les Halles. Here the choices ranged from places where the working men could buy a solid meal in rough surroundings for a few francs, to the odd restaurant with ambitious ideas, sometimes matched by the fare. Between us, Danielle and I had eaten at most of them and shared a consensus on which were worth revisiting.

We found a table in a mid-sized restaurant that looked like it had been in business for over a hundred years without closing. This evening, two large sash windows were open to the street to let air in. The odours of the hot weather in the market came with it, but the bursts of shouting and laughter indicated that no one cared that the rain had begun to spatter the street. Customers were mostly local, or market workers, and were greeted by name as they came and went.

Our table was near the edge of the crowd. No sooner had we sat down but a bottle, two glasses and a basket of bread were noisily placed before us. Menus followed on the waiter's next pass.

I poured the wine and surveyed the room. Fading and peeling green paint covered the walls which had an assortment of panelling, some of which may have been old and quite good. There were brass wall and ceiling lamps, black with age and stained with decades of nicotine.

"They will start serving coffee, bread and hot milk at about two in the morning when the workers come in, with no break in pouring beer and wine," Danielle said. "Then the office workers start coming in and the croissant and brioche will arrive, and the meals and drinking will go on."

We read the creased and worn menu, and Danielle leaned forward and pointed to the heading: Henri IV, 1805.

"Can you imagine what Paris was like then?" she asked. "That's why I love living here."

The food was simple, but good. We exchanged some banter with the waiter who treated us as if he saw us every week, asking about holiday or travel plans in a casual way.

"A few weeks in the Pyrenees," Danielle said. "Enjoying the cooler air, not mountain climbing."

The waiter laughed and moved on.

"Are you really going?" I asked.

"I expect so. My parents like it, and it is good to get out of Paris," she said. "My mother has an old aunt in Poitiers, and my father a cousin near Toulouse, so we take a few days to get down there and a few to get back."

"Will you be able to close the company as usual?" I asked. "We've been so busy."

"By the end of July, it will be quiet," she said. "And you?"

"I don't know. I've nothing planned. I think I'd like to find a small town by a lake or river, not far from Paris," he said. "Somewhere with some good walking, but I don't want to go anywhere in particular."

She laughed.

"Will you take a pile of books? Or perhaps some paints?"

She was teasing, but in truth, she had little idea how I spent my free time, so she hoped this exchange would yield some new information.

"My interests are not particularly intellectual, but I shall have a few books with me," I replied, laughing. "I shall spend my time walking with no purpose and day-dreaming."

"There's only so far one can walk without purpose," Danielle said.

"My purpose will be to return to where I began in time for a good meal," I said. "Does that disappoint you?"

She could see that I was teasing her, too, but I wondered how satisfactorily that would fill my time.

As if reading her thoughts, I added:

"It is quite enough to come to terms with silence," I said. "I still find it nearly overwhelming."

She looked at me sympathetically.

"That is not true only for you, though you come to that feeling from a different experience," she reflected. "I was taught that silence is the voice of God; that can make it almost comforting. I just wish I understood what He was saying."

Our meal arrived and though we hardly spoke as we ate, by the end of the meal, our spirits had revived enough for dessert, coffee and a digestif.

෨

July passed quickly, and Moreau, Doré & Cie. closed at the beginning of the second week in August and Danielle and I went on our separate holidays.

There had been no more concerts, ballets or galleries, and no further contact with Natasha. In fact, things had reverted to the way they had been before she had appeared, though our ease with each other had not diminished. We continued to have a coffee or glass of wine after work, and the occasional meal but the rush to the annual closing preoccupied and exhausted us.

I reflected on the way we worked and met, sitting in shaded groves and by small streams as I wandered my way through August. I wondered if Danielle did, too. It had taken a long time, but I was now enjoying the solitude of the countryside. Though the quiet was no longer frightening, I looked forward to returning to Paris, and finally beginning to live.

From Natasha's Diary

Gargenville

It is always dangerous to write things down, but I am finding it hard to carry all my memories, and while there are many I would gladly part with, the good ones should exist somewhere so others suffering can share the knowledge that even suffering comes to an end.

The last few weeks have been a true respite from life in Paris. Mademoiselle has been very generous, but I have also worked exceptionally hard.

I have a lesson every day and then two hours of practice, usually in the late morning and again in late afternoon after the students who are visiting for the day have left.

As part of my arrangement with Mademoiselle, I work in the kitchen with Sandra, and sometimes her mother, Mme Mercier. She is not a good cook and always criticises poor Sandra, who doesn't argue back and only laughs when her mother leaves. "Poor woman, has nothing else to do," she says.

This is the first time since Aunt Olga died that I have not had to work all day to keep a roof over my head, and it has given me more time to think than I have had since I first left Russia.

Another world; another age.

After three days here, the feeling of peace and safety opened my soul for the first time since those days, and the sadness flowed out. I had to bury my face in the pillows so the whole house didn't hear my sobs.

XII
À la Mode

One of the first things I did on my return from holiday was to move into a new apartment. I'd occupied my one room for nearly four years and now with a good salary, and I believed, good prospects, began looking for a modest apartment at the beginning of the summer.

The areas near work were expensive, and I fancied being somewhere lively; a place that would keep me from becoming as dull as many of my co-workers. They were my colleagues and companions, but stunningly dull, unadventurous, and, worse, uncurious.

A timely chance encounter in a café tipped me off on an apartment in the Rue de Montmorency. I followed it up and found it to offer several good-sized rooms on a third floor corner, so the light was good. It was unfurnished but the landlord was able to put me in touch with a local second-hand furniture dealer to whom he had sold items that had been left behind. In the case of my apartment, only a large *armoire* remained which I duly bought from the landlord.

By the time Danielle returned to Paris, I had collected a bed, a few tables, lamps and a comfortable armchair and moved in.

Though still sparse, and not hugely warm, its convenience to work and space made me think that I could remain there for some time. I was ready to feel settled.

When I returned to work, there was much catching up to be done. Danielle had greeted me warmly and said she looked forward to chatting about our holidays over drinks or dinner. Being the proprietor's daughter gave her the confidence, if not the authority, to make such suggestions. She had time to ask if my summer had been good. I was able to give one or two details, but then she was called away.

While I wanted to see her, I was still sufficiently pleased with my new accommodation to want to spend time in it and think about further improvements. Also, even though it was not far from work, there was a whole new selection of cafés and bistros to explore.

I found shops for groceries and several places to eat and drink. The Café Flamel was tired and traditional compared to the many bright new places that were opening all over Paris. One of the waiters told me that electricity had only been installed the previous year. Still, it was a pleasant place for coffee or *un canon* and the food was good. Over a few weeks I began to recognise locals from the neighbourhood.

Danielle and I resumed meeting for drinks after work

and the odd meal, but I didn't tell her about my new apartment or suggest we visit the Flamel or any of my new haunts. I knew this didn't make much sense and didn't understand it fully myself.

Towards the end of October I was having an evening meal at the Flamel one Saturday and was trying to read the third volume of Proust's reflective novel. I had read the first one in the trenches when there were oceans of idle time, and read the second volume in my quiet seclusion after the Armistice. The mundanity was very attractive in those circumstances and the simple, mis-handled flirtations had a familiarity about them the made me believe life not only could, but would, continue. However, in the bustle of post-war Paris, *Le Côté de Guermantes* felt irrelevant. I felt I owed it to Proust to persevere because he had helped me to survive.

A figure approached my table that I sensed rather than saw, and thinking it was the waiter, marked and closed my book and moved it from my place without looking up. However, the figure, drew out the chair opposite and sat down.

"I told you we went to many of the same places," Natasha said, as the waiter put a glass in front of her.

I poured wine for her and offered her the bread basket. She took a piece, then raised her glass.

"Za zdorov'ye," she said raising her glass.

"Santé."

The waiter gave her a menu and she ordered quickly before chewing a piece of bread.

I watched her, amused, determined not to speak first. I hadn't seen her since the beginning of the summer. She looked well, her face fuller than it had been, and she even had some colour, though she could not be described as looking happy. She wore an old-fashioned dress with mended lace on the collar and had placed a balding sequence handbag on the table. Her hands were very clean and her short nails remained cared for, which suggested her piano playing continued.

"You for get I am a model and used to being stared at," she said when she finished her third piece of bread and was halfway though her second glass of wine.

"Who are you modelling for now?" I asked. "Still M. Du Beaumont?"

She nodded.

"Is his painting any better?" I asked.

She smiled and shook her head.

"No, but he's selling a lot more. There is a growing market for bad painting in Paris," she said.

A small cutlet with a large quantity of boiled potatoes was placed in front of her.

"The new styles of art make it more difficult to tell the good painters from the bad. Unfortunately, that means we have to rely on others to help us make decisions."

"Are you buying now?" I asked.

I was getting used to the dark Russian humour. Pain and suffering were funny. How else could one endure them?

She laughed.

"It helps me choose better painters to pose for," she said. "If I can pose for another Modigliani, I will be able to pose for artists for the rest of my life. What young artist wouldn't love the chance to have a model who posed for a Modigliani. Painters like Du Beaumont could have a tree stump pose for them and no one would know the difference."

"I bet Picasso would like to paint you," I teased.

"I know he would, and not only paint me, but Olga would kill both of us."

She dissected the cutlet with a precision that betrayed her background, whatever it was. No hungry peasant ever cut meat in that manner. Only her focus on eating betrayed her penurious position.

"You haven't been seeing much of Danielle," she said. "You should, you know. She's worried about you."

"I very much doubt that," I said. "Anyway, how would you know what she thinks?"

"I had dinner with her Tuesday," Natasha said. "In the café on Saint Michelle where I saw her before."

This was a talented scrounger. She was much subtler than most, and, now I saw, more calculating. She would get to know the habits of people and cadge drinks and meals. Before the war, I would have been outraged; today, I was happy to help her, and also glad of her company for a short time. I think I would have found her brooding intensity more than I wanted in the long term, but several hours here and there was a pleasant way to carry on.

"How was your summer?" I asked, and hoped it didn't sound condescending or facetious. To my surprise, her face lit up.

"It was wonderful. I had two weeks staying with Mademoiselle outside Paris. It was a very pleasant arrangement: in exchange for room, board, and a daily piano lesson, I worked in the kitchen, served meals and did some light cleaning. I was also able to practice for two hours each day on very good pianos."

I did not know who "Mademoiselle" was, but it sounded an acceptable arrangement and one Natasha appeared to be grateful for.

"And has your playing made great progress?" I asked.

"Yes; I think it has," she said. "It took a while to get out of my bad habits – I shan't embarrass you and tell you what Mademoiselle called them – but once she had me back on track, we moved ahead well. I learned a Ravel piece and she tried to show me how to play Debussy. She says I play everything like Chopin."

She ordered a coffee.

"There's a concert at the beginning of December," she said. "Good Russians, and a piece for the dead of the war that you should hear. Not only the French suffered."

XIII
Rain

Civilian rain was something, even after three years, I was still getting used to. There was something still magical about wearing a mackintosh, carrying an umbrella and even having the option of not going out when it was raining.

There's no point in describing the mud; no one who wasn't there can understand it. Downpours would cause those things that had been carefully isolated to run together and rise under foot and under one's nostrils to create the dread of that thing that was supposed to bring life. Too often, it brought death. It brought death in the diseases it spread, and it literally brought death as once-buried limbs would make a reappearance, giving a grisly wave as they drifted down the sluice.

By contrast, the chestnut scented rain of a Paris spring, or the autumn aroma of wet leaves is unimaginably pleasurable if one could but forget past associations.

November was wet. Possibly the wettest for a number of years and unwelcome memories clashed with the present reality. It was pointless trying to drive back the foul, sodden recollections, just as it was pointless to try to overlay them with happier memories of rain. Indeed, possibly my earliest childhood memory that did not involve faeces was about going into the garden on a bright morning after a night of thunderstorms and smelling the freshness and the ozone – which I am incapable of smelling now – and watching a bumblebee on a rose. The colours of everything seemed so bright: the green of the grass; the blue of the sky; the pink of the flower and the black and yellow of the bee. While it's not been all down hill since then, few memories are as vivid.

The rain in Paris did not affect our business which continued to flourish, nor did it impede the series of activities both work-related and personal. There were visits to customers and potential customers; meetings with shipping and other transport agents, requiring my time at several railway termini which I relished. One meeting had to be suspended briefly as the noise on the roof of the freight shed was so loud that we found ourselves shouting.

The cafés, bistros and restaurants were full and fuggy with windows streaming water, outside from the rain, and inside from the condensation. Danielle and I had finally managed to catch up and had several meals together as well as the more regular coffees and glasses of wine, but I was often tempted just to go home and pull the curtains against the weather.

I had told Danielle about my curious meeting with

Natasha, but did not tell her about the Flamel. On one of the better evenings we walked round to the Opera and bought tickets to the Russian concert Natasha had told me about. We found there was a concert at the end of November with some more familiar – and older – music and bought tickets to that, too.

We talked about going for dinner, but on our way down Rue Quatre Septembre, the heavens opened again. I put Danielle in a convenient taxi and headed for the Metro.

◌

In the following weeks, Natasha did not join me for dinner. Perhaps the rain meant that she was busier as Mme Duflot's clients sought indoor activities. I half expected her to appear to Danielle, but she did not.

Natasha didn't appear at the concert at the Opera at the end of the month. That opulent theatre makes even the worst music bearable, but on this occasion, most of the works were familiar. Maestro Koussevitzky was, once again, welcomed with enormous enthusiasm, though I sensed that the audience – though just as diverse – did not have the preponderance of Russians present. This may have been because the only Russian piece was Prokofiev's *Suite Scythe,* the others – including a soaring performance of the Beethoven Violin Concerto by Jacques Thibaud – being from more Franco-Germanic sources.

Though not a musician, I had, by then, heard enough Prokofiev to recognise his bag of tricks so there was nothing there to surprise me; certainly none of his memorable melodies. It struck me as something of a tug-of-war with Stravinsky with echoes of *Sacre du Printemps*. Imitation or parody? I later learned that Diaghilev who had commissioned it rejected it.

At the time, I kept these thoughts to myself, not having the musical knowledge or vocabulary to express what I meant. Instead, I stated the obvious about the Bach and Beethoven, and Danielle was tolerant.

The performance two weeks later was another story.

This was, again, at the Opera, but this time, the Russians were there in force.

"You can almost smell the borscht," Danielle said as we entered the foyer.

You could certainly smell whatever had been drunk with the vodka. The crowd was exuberant in its expectation and I had the feeling that a number of these people hadn't seen each other since the concert in May.

We had been able to get better seats than for the November concert and sat in the *deuxieme loges de face* on the left side. This gave us a splendid view and Danielle could see a good number of the audience. Periodically, she would pull my arm to point someone out.

Katalsky's *Commemoration Fraternelle,* though not

an immediate favourite, was a thoughtful requiem for the dead of the war, though I was relieved to be on more familiar ground with the pieces by Mussorgsky, Rimsky-Korsakov and Glazunov, who I was told, was a good friend of the conductor.

We looked for Natasha during the interval but failed to find her.

"Charles," Danielle began, pulling me away from watching two pretty girls descending one of the staircases. "Isn't that the man we met at the art gallery?"

She indicated a figure near the wall who was regularly obscured by a cluster of people. It was a curious crowd as it appeared to be a mix of French, Russians, Americans and a few unidentifiable, and possibly Bohemian, patrons.

"He was a Russian, wasn't he?" Danielle asked.

"Some connection with Natasha's family?"

Danielle nodded, as the bell rang for the second half. This offered more Rimsky-Korsakov (the *Vol de Bourdon* provoked joyous laughter at the end) and the Glazunov piece. The final item, by Scriabin, was a fitting bookend to the Katalsky, but I much preferred the contents in between. The Scriabin was, nonetheless, a hit with the audience, though perhaps it was Koussevitzky who was the real object of the near-rapturous reception.

Danielle and I had decided to escape the crowd and leave the area immediately around the Opera for a light supper, and were surprised to find Natasha waiting for us at the foot of the staircase, standing like a statue as the mass of people flowed around her.

"She looks quite lovely," Danielle said as we made our way down. "The angle of her head looking up, and the light on her face is amazing."

"I wonder if anyone's painted her like that."

"My friends!" she exclaimed as she met us.

Making no effort to move from her spot, she embraced Danielle and then offered me her cheeks.

"What a wonderful evening!" she said. "I was quite overcome by it at several points. Were you not moved by the *Commemoration*? And, I thought the chandeliers would come down with *Ei-Oukhniem*."

We had never seen Natasha so animated. Danielle whispered to me that she appeared to have been crying at some point, but now she looked young and happy.

"Come! There are so many friends here."

She took Danielle by the arm and pulled her through the knots of people as I struggled to keep up. Natasha was oblivious to the looks of disapproval of those we collided with and I received most as the last one to career through.

On the steps outside, Natasha joined a group of Russians, few of whom could speak French. She reintroduced us to Vladimir Orloff who was with two American couples, one of which departed within seconds of arrival, seemingly put off by the stream of French and Russian being rained on them.

The other American couple appeared to be friends of Orloff. We were introduced and both spoke French well, but with very American accents. Other Russians appeared to be pushing to leave for food, drink, or both and Orloff and Natasha succeeded in sweeping us up into their group; we walked, swaying and laughing, and barely paying attention to where we were.

XIV
Scorched Earth

There is a myth that the reason we talk of drinking *un canon de vin* is from a Masonic tradition of drinking all at once then banging the glasses on the table simultaneously, making a sound that echoes around the room. Others maintain that it's related to drinking the measure in one go, or shot. I had always presumed these explanations to be fanciful, though they occupied time in the officer's mess during the brief times such pleasures were possible. Given the 16th century origins of the expression, I always felt it more likely to refer to the similar shape of the mouths. Then again, I was susceptible to believing the tale of the shape of the *coupe de champagne*.

That night, however, when we found ourselves crammed into a smoky Russian bar, with *"Kartofel"* painted over the door, I revised my opinion. The noise of explosions of vodka glasses slammed on the tables were frequent and loud enough to lead me to imagine General Kutuzov himself giving the command.

Amid the drinking, various dishes of food arrived. Danielle and I did not understand any of the Russian being spoken and were seated at one of several tables holding ten or so people. Natasha moved about the room until the food arrived. There were baskets of bread, and bowls of potato soup and baked potatoes.

It seemed that anyone who left the table lost his place, and possibly his food and drink. That did not stop a continuous rotation of people that at one point brought Natasha, Orloff and the American couple to our table. They were immaculately dressed and everything they wore was of a high quality, but not necessarily of a high price (Danielle later told me). Their impeccable dress did not make them fussy, or anything but engaging and seemingly willing to join in the fun. The wife, named Sara, engaged Danielle in conversation while Orloff, Gerald and I were part of a discussion about the opera house, led by Natasha.

"In a building so wonderfully extravagant, why is the ceiling of the auditorium so dull?" she asked.

"Perhaps that's why Pablo was there," Orloff suggested.

We laughed loudly and were interrupted by another toast and barrage of vodka glasses.

"An interesting ceiling would give one something to look at during the ballet," Sara said, unexpectedly joining the conversation.

The good humour continued until Orloff and the Murphys rose and moved to another table.

"Thank you for including us in your party," Murphy

said to me as he left.

"Nothing to do with me."

"Only if you get stuck with the bill," he said, and they left the bar.

A useful piece of advice, considering the accomplishment with which a certain Russian young lady deployed the tactic.

Both Natasha and Danielle had consumed more than I'd seen either drink. Through some surreptitious spilling and reuse of an empty glass (a useful trick and a good excuse for a jacket with large pockets), I remained in better shape than most. I also recognised the wisdom of Murphy's warning.

Natasha pulled my arm over as I looked at my watch, muttered something in Russian, and we all beat a retreat as another fusillade echoed about us.

As I feared, the sudden blast of cold air had a stupefying effect on Danielle, who gasped, wobbled and leaned against me in rising confusion. Natasha had headed off in the opposite direction after pinching Danielle's cheeks affectionately.

"It's about time you had some real fun," she giggled.

I began walking south-east in the hope of finding a café that might let us in as I could not return Danielle to her parents as she was, nor was there anyway she'd make it up the stairs to my apartment.

Fortunately, as she walked, her head cleared and her balance improved. She tried not to cling to me as much as she had been, but was forced to reconciling herself to the fact that she'd have to continue to hold on for the foreseeable future.

Eventually, we reached the familiar area of Les Halles with its ever-open bars, cafés and restaurants. We found a modest bistro where we had never been (no doubt is ruining reputations at this stage) and found a table in a dim corner.

"I'm so sorry," Danielle whispered.

I laughed.

"What for?"

"I must look like something you picked up on the Boulevard Saint Denis."

"Here."

I pushed the hot coffee towards her.

"Do you want me to hold the cup for you?" I asked.

"Not funny," she said, picking it up unsteadily.

"I hope neither of us remembers any of this in the morning," she said, with something of her self-parody returning.

"It was a memorable evening. And the concert was excellent."

"Did we go to a concert?"

From Natasha's Diary

It is very odd to think that more than half my short life has been lived in exile. I cannot help thinking sometimes how different my life would be, but that's just vanity and I have proved that I can survive.

Life continues to move away from the war and the revolution and each day it's harder to remember lost friends and my dear, dear family. I continue to have nothing, but I have my life, reasonable health and as much freedom as I can afford. Perhaps 1922 will be more prosperous.

I still need to take care. Those who would harm me continue to gather in Paris and are becoming more organised, placing those of us who would prefer peaceful lives in danger. You can hardly go to a restaurant without being waited on by a Grand Duchess or Duke. The nobility that has money has done so little for those who do not that it is almost possible to empathise with the Bolsheviks.

This is dangerous to write and I must stop.

It is already March and I have cut myself off from too many friends. That one evening of old revelry could easily have been my undoing. My dear Charles and Danielle certainly think I am feckless and unreliable. They have been kind and not asked for anything from me. Charles might if he doesn't realise how much he loves Danielle soon. I must keep Vladimir at arm's length, though he now moves with people I would like to know.

Mademoiselle continues to be good to me and I am learning so much. There is much good new music in Paris. She has already suggested that I come to Gargenville again on the same basis this summer.

If only to be normal and not remember what I do.

XV
Le Sacre du Printemps

As businesses became increasingly buoyant, so did the fortunes of Moreau, Doré et Cie. The office expanded to several rooms on an upper floor, and various rearrangements were made, the significant result of this was that I was now sharing a private office with Danielle.

From a business point of view, it made good sense as our work complemented each other: essentially, I was buying, and she was distributing. We now had a few people working under us, so there was constant traffic in and out of our office.

We were both amused by the obvious manipulation, but were comfortable enough with each other to shrug it off.

With spring, our moods again lifted and we spent as much time outside as possible. We'd gone to a few galleries and to the Louvre, but had not encountered Natasha. We speculated that she was involved with a new lover/painter and absorbed with that.

There was a Koussevitzky concert at Trocadero in March, and though the music looked good, it was a benefit concert for the starving in Russia, sponsored by the

League of the Rights on Man and of the Citizen. That in itself did not put us off, but there were also three addresses in the programme that both Danielle and I thought we could do without. There was also the possibility of unrest which we were also anxious to avoid.

Did that make us uncaring? Cowards? I think we felt that we'd made sufficient sacrifices for a lifetime, though we made small cash contributions.

The War was still around us. Wounded soldiers begging; refugees looking for homes and work, driven to the margins of the city. In spite of the growing prosperity of individual enterprises, the state remained burdened with war debt and a failing infrastructure, but the gaiety, music and laughter rode on top of it all.

I continued to have accidental personal encounters with men I had served with; their widows or grieving parents who would recognise me as an old acquaintance and tell me their stories. I helped where I could, but it was never much. Several of these people became part of my routine, and I'd visit them every month or two.

One officer's widow was so desperate to have a father for her son that she offered me free room and board just so there would be a man in the child's life. When I told Danielle, she began to weep. I didn't see how I could continue to visit without raising false expectations. Danielle understood, but thought that cutting them out of my life would be unnecessarily cruel.

Her solution was that the next time I wanted to visit them that she come with me. The widow was taken aback by Danielle's presence, but we took her and the child to a meal one Saturday, and the following month, we were both invited to a meal at their home. We continued that alternation of meals until a few years later when the widow found a new husband.

I found myself drinking coffee or wine with damaged soldiers whom I barely knew. Often, little was said; it was enough to be with someone who understood.

I mention these things lest these years are seen as overly glamorous. While brilliant and exciting, it was no golden age. Once the poems and novels began to appear, the extent of the trauma on the psyche became more apparent. Not just the national psyche, but on that of all nations who had participated. In the UK, the land of the dramatists, only one play about the war was ever produced, such was the inability to recreate it.

ဆ

Sharing an office with Danielle had the effect of reducing the time we spent together away from it. At least twice a week we'd go for a drink, and dinner every fortnight, but these were spontaneous not planned encounters. We hardly ever saw each other on weekends now but neither of us suspected the other had a secret romantic interest. I went for long walks, often following the river. Few bits of it within the city were attractive; mostly, it was industrial and I'd sit and watch barges being unloaded while enjoying a cigarette. I'd drink in the bars and listen to conversations about the river, the boats, how busy they were and how they hated their bosses, captains, landlords, and wives.

Occasionally, I'd be drawn into a conversation and would learn a lot about the shipment of beer, wine, tomatoes, furniture, machinery and fish. Fish was often the main topic, and I began to be able to tell which industries favoured a bar by smell. However, it was in an establishment off Quai Bercy that I encountered Luc Barnard.

He had been in the same company with me in the War. We met early on in our time in uniform, and although he was a private soldier and I a shiny new *sous-lieutenant*, we were the same. Though we didn't often have a chance to chat, we kept an eye on each other; shared cigarettes, chocolate, a joke, or a few extra bullets.

These days, veterans like us were easy to spot. In the first place, there weren't many of us and, we were told, we shared the same haunted look. I hadn't realised it, but I had taken to looking for fellows my age in cafés and bars; it was Luc who brought it to my attention.

"Charles! What brings you to Place Pinard?" he called to me as I ordered a drink.

He approached with a smile and rough handshake, but, in truth, he looked little better than when I'd seen him in the trenches.

We moved down the bar where there was a small space.

"I'm still in the 'long walk' phase," I said. "I find myself in some very curious places."

He nodded as his customary gloom settled back over his face.

"It's a funny thing being able to move at will," he said. "Has it made you fearless, too?"

I knew what he meant. I was unafraid; I had no particular ability to defend myself, but I was afraid of nothing the city had to offer.

"I did the walks, too," Luc resumed. "But then, I needed to work – to live, and to drag myself back into life. I'm on and off the barges now. Up the river and down, rolling endless barrels of good wine and bad. It's been good to keep moving, though my father wants me to get serious about the business. He says I know the bottom of the barrel now and should move to an office.

"*La fin de la rêverie de la rivière,*" he said with a sad sigh, then added, "*Mais, pas la fin du vin!*"

He sounded content, but not happy. A familiar situation. I was about to say something when a friend of his joined us with his drink. I thought he looked familiar but couldn't place him.

"One of my shipmates," Luc said. "Ilya."

I shook hands with Ilya, who smiled and nodded.

"Luc was telling me about his travels," I said.

Ilya nodded.

"We've become drinking buddies," Luc said. "There's not much about wine that Ilya doesn't know – and he makes a good beef stew."

"Do barges have cooks?"

Luc and Ilya laughed.

"On occasion we take turns cooking if there's no inn near by," Ilya said.

"That we haven't been thrown out of, he means," Luc added.

I suddenly recognised Ilya.

"You were at the bar after the concert," I said to Ilya in recognition. His accent triggered my memory. "*Kartofel.*"

Ilya looked uncertain, then smiled.

"I'm surprised you can remember anything about that night," he said with a hearty laugh.

Luc looked very confused, but Ilya explained our encounter to him.

"You are friends with the Russians in Paris?" Ilya asked, returning to his more cautious demeanour.

"With some," I said.

"Be very careful," he said, finishing his drink. "Some of us are very dangerous to know. Not me; not to you, at least. But, there is a growing number of wolves in sheep's clothing who will make trouble."

He clapped his hand on my arm and left.

Luc and I exchanged puzzled looks.

"There's a rumour that he's an exiled count," he said.

From Natasha's Diary

It's summer again and I am here again. Mademoiselle is again being very kind. She said I hadn't lost too much ground over the year and that my technique was still good. I know what that really means, but it's all I have time for except when I'm here.

It's hard to believe that a year has gone by; everything is so familiar. Sandra's abilities and confidence as a cook have grown, and it is now very pleasant to work with her. She is also more able to cope with her mother telling her that she's doing everything wrong. I admire her patience.

I feel safe here. It's only a few miles from Paris, but it's a different world. Unfortunately, there is no way I could earn a living outside Paris. Du Beaumont is gone and in March I had to find somewhere else to live.

For a while, I thought I would have to make another withdrawal from my bank. I don't know how long it will last. I have made four withdrawals in the past five years. I can only make eight more. I will still be less than thirty.

There was a lot of work earlier to get the costumes ready for "La Belle au Bois Dormant" for the London pro-duction so I could delay the withdrawal and afford to take a room with some students in Rue du Cardinal Lemoine.

The students are noisy and argue all the time, but they are pleased with life, which Du Beaumont and most other painters are not.

The Irishman was different; he was a contented man; a craftsman with no grand illusions. All he wanted to do was the best work he could; he didn't seem to worry about the future, only the pieces he was working on. All he wanted from me was show up on time, hold my pose and be still.

He talked while he formed the model and I learned a lot about how he thought; how he felt about his work, other artists (he said Rodin never put chisel to marble in his life; it was all done by apprentices). He told me about the Irish writers, too. He wasn't as amusing as Modigliani, Du Beaumont, or even Soutine on a good day, more in the gentlemanly way of Degas.

Stop. I mustn't look back. We had a diversion yesterday when Georges Auric and Francis Poulenc came by. Mademoiselle, though teaching, received them, and they disrupted everyone's morning with their playing and joking. In the end Mademoiselle joined them playing duets and improvisations. She told Poulenc that his piano technique was dreadful and threatened to hit his knuckles with a ruler, at which point, he began playing music hall and bar room songs that she called "ragtime."

We gave them lunch – they had brought a good deal

of wine – and she pushed them out the door, with much laughter. I had never seen Mademoiselle laugh so much and suspect she hasn't since her sister died.

I remarked that they were amusing, and that M. Poulenc's tunes while curious were pleasing.

"If you want to hear more of them, go to La Boeuf sur la Toite. They all hang out there."

I thought they would be people Charles and Danielle would enjoy seeing. They had liked the music to Les Marié de la Tour Eiffel. I've barely seen them this year. I didn't dare return to the Flamel. Charles is so patient and kind; he pities me, and I can't accept it. He is also close to seeing me for who I am, not that it seems to bother him.

Apart from that evening after the concert (I hope Danielle has forgiven me; she seems to have) I only saw them once, by accident in the Jardin du Luxembourg. We had a drink and Charles told me he had seen Ilya. Such encounters are not good. And the talk of Grand Duchess Anastasia showing up in Berlin is very disturbing, though it certainly cannot be true.

XVI
Falling Leaves

Since it is Natasha who is the subject of this recollection, it is not necessary to do more than sketch in those bits of my life, and Danielle's, that are needed to help connect the dots.

Danielle and I continued to work together and her father and the other directors continued to let us expand our responsibilities. We were both still very young so no sudden promotions to major decision-making would come our way, nor did we want more than we were doing. Our work gave us the time to enjoy the theatre and restaurants as well as continue our inexpert forays into galleries and concerts.

We made a number of visits to the Louvre, eventually focusing on individual collections and periods. It was too easy for things to become a blur and did nothing to increase our knowledge or enjoyment. We also made several trips to Versailles which, perhaps after the turmoil of the war, seemed even more a relic of an age that was increasingly hard to imagine.

Danielle spent nearly an hour in the hall of mirrors, walking as if in a trance repeatedly from one end to the other, staring into the mirrors at her reflection as she passed. I let her move on her own and sauntered into the adjoining rooms which I believed to be tasteless.

I didn't know whether she fancied herself as Maria Theresa or Marie Antoinette. I believed that to do so would have been out of character and her walk and posture suggested that she had no such thoughts, yet she looked into the mirrors and out the windows as though transported.

I waited at one end of the hall and she eventually joined me and we went into the gardens, but she was ready to leave.

"There's a café near the station," she said, and we walked to the exit as the crowds continued to flood in.

It wasn't yet time for lunch, so we ordered croissants with our coffee.

I wasn't going to be the first to make a comment on the palace. I'd said most of what I thought on previous visits.

"Let's do the galleries around Rue Royale," she suggested. "The one where you met Natasha and the one she took us to – and any others."

We returned to Paris, hardly talking. Danielle was looking out the window for most of the journey back. We walked from the station to Rue Royale and the Galerie Hébrard. Danielle paused to stare into Place de la

Concorde. I assumed she was contemplating the fate of those who had come from where we had just been.

"Listening for the tumbrils?" I asked.

"It's hard to really feel for anyone in history," she said. "We learn about it at school, and read the stories and novels, but they're not people; they are characters, whether in a history book or a novel."

"That's what you were doing in the hall," I said, gently. She nodded.

"Just as those mirrors reflected me, they reflected those people from history who walked there, or danced." I was trying to get a sense of their reality – which is why I wanted to come this way," she said.

She look around at the grand buildings and the obelisk and shook her head sadly.

"Nothing?"

"No," she whispered. "Suffering loss, I thought I might be able to feel something."

She took my arm and we walked to the gallery.

ം

We didn't get to the Rosenberg gallery that day, but a curious encounter at the concert in November drew unexpected threads together.

Natasha had found Danielle at a dry goods store and told her to be sure to attend the next Russian concert in November. Danielle said that Natasha appeared to be in a hurry, but said she'd be there along with other people Danielle may – or may not – remember.

The "may not" was Danielle's embellishment. She was still reluctant to talk about (or remember) the aftermath of the previous visit to l'Opera.

We followed Natasha's instructions and bought our tickets. The concert was on a Thursday and it was obvious from the programme that it would be a late evening.

"We have to work in the morning, so there will be no carousing and singing the 'Volga Boatmen' with Russian *emigrés* and refugees at *Kartofel*," said Danielle in her stern employer's voice.

She was right about one thing: it wasn't at *Kartofel*.

∝

We arrived at the theatre at about twenty to nine. Danielle squeezed my arm. Entering that palace was always exciting, and we looked forward to another rousing concert made memorable by Prokofiev himself playing his third piano concerto.

As before, Russians dominated the crowd, but the division between them was more marked than ever: the workers and the aristocracy were ranged at different ends of the grand foyer, and soon migrated to different levels of the auditorium. While there was tension between them, virtually all of them had been supporters of the tsar and now were in shared exile.

We scanned the crowd as we ascended the staircase, not expecting to see anyone we knew, but I saw Ilya talking to some friends while Danielle saw Natasha coming up the stairs to meet us.

"Come!" she said, urgently, taking us both by the arm and leading us to a space behind two columns on the mezzanine.

Danielle shot me an "it's going to be another one of *those* evenings" looks, but I was more taken by Natasha's looks than of any impending crisis. She looked healthier than I had seen her; her cheeks were no longer hollow. Her features looked refined and she was wearing her rich auburn hair in a more fashionable style and even had some carefully applied make-up. I wondered if it was a new artist or lover who was behind this more affluent appearance.

Danielle refused to be intimidated by the theatricality.

"We are looking forward to the evening," she said, conversationally. "It looks like you are, too."

She tried to smile at Danielle, but her eyes kept darting to the staircase and the floor below.

"There is a rumour that Kirill Vladimirovich is coming tonight," she whispered darkly. "He must not see me."

Danielle smiled gently.

"We'll take care of you, Natasha."

Natasha shook her head.

"No. No one can."

Danielle seized Natasha by the shoulders and gave her a light shake. It surprised me as much as it did Natasha.

"Now, listen, young lady," she said forcefully, but smiling and glancing at the passing crowd. "This is Paris. We're going to a concert. There are thousands of people around. Now, stop this silliness; nothing is going to happen to you. Where is your seat? Charles can take it and you can sit with me in the *deuxieme loges*."

Natasha appeared stunned by the admonition that made me think Danielle would have made an exceptional school mistress.

"Have you seen Prokofiev perform before?" she asked in normal tones before Natasha could recover.

"I've seen him with the Ballet Russes. Sometimes he plays the piano, but I've never seen him in concert," she said. "Stravinsky is here, too."

"A memorable evening," Danielle said.

"I must go to my seat," Natasha said.

"You meet us here – right here – during the interval. Charles will have a glass of wine for you," Danielle told her.

"Yes, ma'am," Natasha replied, and gave the hint of a curtsey before walking quickly towards the stairs.

Danielle and I looked at each other in disbelief.

"She didn't learn *that* on a farm."

XVII
Prokofiev, Stravinsky & Mussorgsky

1922

F ew people ever experience or witness the kind of rap-
turous adulation – even adoration – that was poured
out to Koussevitzky that evening. Prokofiev even caught
some of it. From the moment he appeared on the vast
stage, Koussevitzky dominated the evening. Everything
fell under his control. Even Prokofiev. Even Stravinsky,
but especially Mussorgsky.

At the time, my musical sophistication was in its
formative stage, but with the benefit of age, I now realise
(as have others who have written about those days), that
this specific evening was the point where the pre- and
post-revolutionary Russian music fused. The concert included the premiere of two French pieces and an impres-
sive suite by Stravinsky, but it was with the performance
of the Prokofiev piano concerto that fired the auditorium.

The third piano concerto had been premiered in the
United States to a mixed reaction. No doubt there had
been some tinkering in the meantime, but the combination of the music, Prokofiev's playing, Koussevitzky's
verve and the readiness of the audience to be astounded
(Diaghilev's notion) that cemented the concerto as part

of the foundation of 20th century music.

The noise in the grand foyer during the interval was extraordinary. There was an almost celebratory atmosphere as people looked for friends to share their comments. While the French were grouped in intimate clusters, the Russians appeared to be organising themselves by the geographic region of their origin.

I was less certain than Danielle that Natasha would join us, but I collected a glass of champagne for her anyway. It was a luxury for us, but we, too, bourgeois French, had been caught up in the magic.

"Wasn't that spectacular!" Natasha exclaimed. "What a piece!"

She took the champagne from my hand and drank.

"There are people from the ballet here; pupils of Mademoiselle, and other acquaintances," she said, looking down on the main crowd.

"I saw Ilya earlier," I said.

Natasha looked at me cautiously.

"Did you speak to him?"

"He didn't see me."

Sensing danger, Danielle interrupted.

"Do you suppose that American couple is here?"

"Vladimir's friends who we met at the gallery?" Natasha, asked brightly. "It wouldn't surprise me."

We drank in silence then Natasha spoke to Danielle.

"I am sorry for my earlier behaviour," she said, almost returning to her schoolgirl demeanour. "I had a shock and was not myself."

Danielle said nothing, but squeezed her hand and smiled.

"Can you tell us?" I asked.

Danielle looked disapprovingly at me, but I ignored her and turned to Natasha, waiting for a reply.

She looked worried for a moment, but the electric atmosphere of this momentous occasion persuaded her to reply.

"Does the name Kirill Vladimirovich mean anything to you?" she asked.

We shook our heads.

"He betrayed his cousin to save his skin," she said. "He swore allegiance to the provisional government when he should have defended our beloved Nicholas.

"Since the Bolsheviks took over, he is now in France and has a growing following. Not only that, he is taking measures to ensure that he is the acknowledged leader of those loyal to the Romanoffs. I believe that he is systematically eliminating those who would challenge him.

She went quiet and looked down, then faced us and whispered.

"He won't pay attention to me, but his supporters don't want me around," she said softly.

"You make it sound like a secret army," I said.

"It is, and it's going to get worse," she said.

Danielle was about to ask something when the bell rang for the second half.

"Meet me here afterwards," Natasha said.

Prokofiev was back with two pieces from *The Love of Three Oranges* to open the second half and then came *Pictures at an Exhibition*. I don't think that even people who knew the piano version were prepared for Ravel's orchestration. It certainly didn't sound French to me.

From the opening trumpet *motif* to the thunderous chords of the "Great Gate of Kiev" with the brass, tympani and bells piercing the luxury of the ocean of strings with an orchestration worthy of Rimski-Korsakov.

The sound echoed in absolute silence for at least five seconds before Maestro Koussevitzky dropped his arms and turned to the audience which rose with joy as if it had just received news of a victory in war. The ovation continued as he made repeated returns to the podium for nearly fifteen minutes.

These comments are not mine, of course, but bits I collected subsequently. Still, I could see for myself the tears in the eyes of many who seemed to feel that they had been momentarily transported back to the Russia they had known.

Even Danielle was breathless, wondering what she

had just heard.

A large number of the audience remained in place even as the musicians left the stage as if they expected a sudden return of the Maestro for another burst of lost patriotic dreams. Eventually, when that expectation was unfulfilled, the audience, though not the noise, dissipated.

Danielle and I watched from our seats until the aisle behind us was clear. I had totally forgotten about meeting Natasha, but Danielle nudged me towards the appointed location. She was there and appeared to be glowing.

I started to ask how she liked it, but she put her finger to my lips.

"Don't make me leave that world yet," she said. "Come."

We followed her out of the building and walked a short distance down Avenue de l'Opera. Unexpectedly, she waved to a taxi and we got in. I mentally calculated how much money I had with me, well aware of the girl's *modus operandi*.

"Rue Littré; the Rue de Rennes end," she said with more confidence than I'd heard from her before.

She sat back in the seat with us.

"I want you to meet some friends," she said.

I looked at Danielle to see if she knew Rue Littré. But she shook her head. Rue de Rennes was a long road that ran from Boulevard Saint Germain into the Montparnasse district.

The taxi made countless turns once across the river and there were no landmarks that I could recognise. It was nearly eleven-thirty and there were still people in the streets; the bistros and cafés were lit up though the crowds were thinning. I remembered it was Thursday and Danielle and I would have to be at work on time in the morning. Well, at least I would.

"Rue Littré," the driver said.

We got out, and I paid the driver.

Natasha had said nothing in the taxi apart from humming fragments of the Mussorgsky.

"This way."

We followed her down the street and she opened a door into a typical courtyard and started up the steps. We went up to the second floor, walked nearly halfway around the passage and she knocked loudly on a door.

It was opened in a moment by an elderly butler who let us in.

"*Spasibo*, Kornenko."

It seemed that Kornenko was about to speak, but checked himself, bowed deeply and stood back to admit us into the apartment.

It was an elegant and richly furnished set of large rooms with high ceilings, panelling and ornate plaster.

Natasha walked along the hallway confidently and turned into a drawing room where a fire burned and a handsome couple in late middle age moved forward to greet her. The man bent towards her and kissed her hand, then she and the woman gave the hint of a curtsy to each other. During this dumbshow, Danielle and I turned to each other, silently querying the curious Russian custom. Then, the three of them suddenly relaxed, and with big smiles and exclamations, embraced and kissed each other's cheeks, after which Natasha turned to us.

"Danielle and Charles, may I please introduce you to Prince Alex and Princess Anya ~~Karpov~~." Rostov.

XVIII
Pretences

Somehow, Danielle and I made it to the office by nine Friday morning. While remarkable, the greater mystery was how we got home the previous night. After our official introduction, the "prince and princess" were referred to as "Uncle André" and "Aunt Anya" by Natasha, though they explained that there was no relationship between them. Indeed, they had not known each other in Russia.

"I met Aunt Anya at Mademoiselle's when I was there for a lesson about four years ago," Natasha said. "Aunt Anya was looking for someone to play duets with and given our common heritage and fate, Mademoiselle felt we'd get along. It would be good for me to play with a better player, too."

Shortly after, the champagne started, and I needed to compare notes with Danielle to determine what happened after that. Once she had cleared her urgent morning business, Danielle suggested early drinks – after all, it was a Friday afternoon.

"Why does champagne make one so thirsty?" she asked me as we walked to *L'Homme d'Affaires*.

"I don't know about you but I'm exhausted," she continued as we sat down. "It was all I could do to concentrate today. I'm going to have a light supper and sleep all weekend."

We were served our customary glasses of wine and tried to reassemble the previous evening.

"We did get a chance to hear Natasha play the piano," I said.

"How big was that apartment?" Danielle asked. "When we first entered that room, I failed two notice two grand pianos."

"There were two? Oh, good. I was afraid I was seeing double," I said. "I guess the other player was Princess Anya."

Danielle laughed.

"Don't pretend! We were still on the first bottle when they played."

"Mozart!" we both said together.

Danielle nodded.

"Things may not have been as bad as we feared," I said. "We haven't forgotten everything."

"They were charming," Danielle said. "They didn't know us, and there was that lovely buffet."

As we discussed it, we concluded that our problems didn't start until we went out into the fresh air at what must have been close to two-thirty.

"My father said he was about to ring the police," Danielle laughed. "Mother stopped him. This morning, her fear had turned to anger; she said that at the time she'd rather I was found dead than 'disgraced.'"

Mme Doré was *formidable*, but in a way that was amusingly vague and eccentric. Still, it couldn't have been a pleasant breakfast for Danielle being berated and hung-over.

"Apart from the music, there was a lot of political discussion, wasn't there?" Danielle asked.

"There was talk of that Kirill Vladimirovich. André seemed to think he was at the concert."

"Oh, it's 'André,' is it? You must have got on very well," Danielle teased. "Though, after playing the piano with Anya, Natasha monopolised him."

"The conversation kept drifting in and out of Russian," I said. "Natasha was the one to slip into it. André tried to keep me in the conversation."

"*Noblesse oblige.*"

Danielle's mordant manner was returning.

"They were talking about the aristocrats aligning with Kirill, closing ranks among the exiled, and squeezing out those they feel are their opponents or imposters," I said.

Danielle drank and thought.

"Why would that be a concern to the prince?" she asked. "Surely it would be easy to prove. There must be people who would recognise him."

I shook my head.

"Just Russian gossip," Danielle added.

"I don't think so. They sounded far too serious," I said. "I suppose there are a lot of them. That chap, Ilya, who was at the *Kartofel* that night – "

"*Don't!*" Danielle protested, covering her eyes with her hand, and laughing.

"I saw him while I had a drink with my army friend, Luc. He recognised me and joined us. Luc said he was a count before the revolution."

"Do you think he was?"

"That was the other thing that Natasha said last night; it was while they were speaking in Russian. She said that word again, 'Okhrana.'"

"Is that what it was?"

"André repeated it, but quickly stopped Natasha from going further and asked me in English how I had liked the Prokofiev concerto."

"Russians!" Danielle said, dismissively. "I just want to go to the theatre; I don't want to get caught up in another revolution."

"I'll ask her to explain when we next see her."

☙

Of course, we didn't see Natasha for another six months.

Danielle and I were in another busy time for the company, and then there was the break for Christmas. While it didn't last long, it disrupted the rhythm of things.

The Dorés invited me for Christmas lunch. I declined, but at the time had no better offer. Unexpectedly, one Saturday afternoon, Luc knocked on my door. We went to a café and then to dinner, and then to several more cafés of declining salutiferocity.

We ate and drank and talked nonsense about nothing. There were no reminiscences; no reflections on the war; no moaning about our jobs, and the night (or early morning) culminated in an invitation to go to his family for Christmas dinner. He contacted me a week later, stone cold sober, to repeat the invitation, lest I thought it was a drunken gesture.

It was a pleasant day. I took several bottles of wine and made my way to Quai de Bercy and the tangled streets and alleys between the river and the marshalling yards of Gare de Lyon. I felt stupid bringing three bottles of wine to the neighbourhood through which nearly every drop consumed in Paris passed.

Luc's family had a good-sized house on four floors. The ground floor had been flooded in the inundation of 1910 and remained sparsely furnished, but the upstairs drawing room was comfortable and Luc's father, mother, sister and a cousin, Jean, who was about our age, were welcoming.

The family had come from Burgundy several generations earlier and the festivity's food and drink reflected that region. My bottles were not unappreciated, though from Bordeaux.

Luc's father was a senior clerk for one of the many wine distributors in the area and he clearly hoped that Luc would soon abandon his labouring life and take up an office job, for which he was well-suited.

Mme Barnard ensured everything was ready, in order, and properly served – without making a fuss. Conversation was lively and affectionate. I found M. Barnard a very jolly man for one who spent his life totting up figures and processing orders and deliveries.

As I thought this, the recognition that I had just described my own life hit me like a slap across the face. Only Simone noticed that I had become suddenly distracted.

She was a few years younger than Luc and me and gave the impression that she could be pretty. She was petite and could probably pass for a sixteen-year-old. I mentally compared her to Natasha, as their age was similar, but the simple joy that permeated Simone's every sentence marked them as quite different creatures.

It was something of a family joke that she also worked in the wine business, but not for the same firm as her father. There was no competition as his trade was wholesale and hers to the restaurant trade.

"Papa sells by the barrel, I sell by the case," she explained.

"Simone pours wine for all the *sommeliers* in Paris," Mme Barnard said.

"And finishes what they don't," Luc added, to laughter.

She made an impatient wave at him, and laughed, too.

"Let's see what you make of what Charles brought," Luc said, half way through the meal.

"Let's not embarrass people," Mme Barnard said.

I glanced at M. Barnard who was thoroughly enjoying watching his family tease each other.

Luc fetched one of my bottles from the sideboard and handed it to Simone.

"Here you are; show us what you can do," he said.

She took the bottle and applied the corkscrew and carefully placed the cork on a saucer. She took a clean glass, placed it before her father and expertly poured the amount for sampling.

They went through this ritual perfectly seriously, but Luc caught my eye and wordlessly signalled that this was a game they enjoyed.

M Barnard smelled the cork, then cut it in half and inspected it. He then turned to the glass, swirled the wine and sniffed it. A mischievous glance at Simone confirmed what Luc had indicated. He then tasted it and made a face.

"*Ce n'est pas Bourgogne, mais c'est peut-être français. Maintenant, arrête de déconner et remplis mon verre,*" he said, then laughed loudly.

It was fun, and I was grateful for the tip-off.

"Perhaps this will make up for it," I said to Luc and handed him a book wrapped in brown paper.

Siegfried et le Limousin had appeared that year. I thought it might amuse him.

Simone sat back down and looked at me.

"Next year, you must bring *me* a present, too."

XIX
Another Spring

As I said, we didn't see Natasha again for months. Ordinary people would have checked to see if their inebriated friends had made it home safely; explained why they were dragged across Paris to meet André and Anya; or just generally chatted about the evening.

It was a topic that Danielle and I returned to from time to time over coffee or a glass of wine.

"At least we got to hear her play the piano," I said, when we met for a drink on a cold Friday evening in early March. "I always wondered how good she was."

Danielle was quiet, and I asked her why.

She made a motion, brushing aside the question.

"I'm just a little off balance," she said.

"Are you feeling all right?"

"Oh, yes; I'm fine. I'm thinking too much, that's all," she said, dismissively.

This wasn't the sort of thing Danielle usually said. While she may not have been a thinker in the eyes of a philosopher, she did have a well organised and disciplined mind, so I was not content with her response. However, it was not the time to challenge her, so I changed topics. I asked her how she thought one of our new clerks was fitting in. The business continued to expand and even with a lot of people wanting jobs, Moreau, Doré et Cie. had difficulty in finding staff who "could sustain an interest in grain powders" as one man had said when giving his notice.

M. Moreau said that most people found an interest in being paid regularly, but the man was not persuaded.

"The girls stay longer," Danielle commented, "but not long-term. They like being able to afford to buy things and be seen wherever they want to be seen. We're just a means to an end. Few will be here for more than a year –

"Charles, this isn't what I want to talk about," she said not loudly, but with some force, which caught me off guard.

She drank the rest of her wine and stood up.

"I'll see you Monday," she said and was out of the café before I could stand.

She said it in her neutral business voice and didn't sound cross with me, but what was at the root of her behaviour was a mystery. All I knew is that I had been looking forward to dinner with her – though nothing had been formally agreed – and perhaps some outing over the weekend. As it was, I'd need to ensure I had enough coal to stay at home and rely on Proust to keep me entertained.

౪

I wasn't sure what I'd find Monday morning when I went to work, but everything seemed normal, if not entirely relaxed. Given the amount of time Danielle and I spent together, despite our obvious intentions for nothing serious or lasting, it was probably for the best that a more professional distance re-established itself.

On a Saturday in March, when the battle against winter was nearly over, and Paris was losing its dead smells and spring had claimed a secure foothold, Luc found me in a café in Rue du Temple near my apartment. He was with Simone and another young lady. They were laughing as they looked in the window and saw me with my solitary beer and the remains of lunch, and waved and made faces.

"You look so miserable!" he exclaimed coming in.

They collected chairs, took off their coats and settled down. Luc went to the bar to order a bottle of wine. Simone introduced me to Honorine, who was attractive if undemonstrative. I had supposed she was a friend of Simone until the patron arrived with a bottle of *Crémant d'Alsace* and four flutes.

"Charles, *mon vieux*, I am engaged to marry this lovely lady," he said. "It is wonderful to be happy, even though I am giving up life on the river to work in an office."

We toasted them and Simone continued the narrative.

"I was at school with Honorine," she said. "We'd lost

touch until shortly before Christmas when I found her again when I was shopping; she was selling scarves at Franck et Fils."

"I was invited home to dinner. I understand you know what that's like," Honorine said. "I hadn't seen Luc since before – well, in a long time."

The skirting of the mention of the war was not lost on me, and we all knew that the world to which Honorine referred no longer existed.

"We met for a drink, then dinner, then – " Luc related enthusiastically.

"I'm sure Charles gets the idea," Honorine said.

"I'm sure he does," Simone added, leaning against me and taking my arm.

I suddenly understood Danielle's uncharacteristic mood. Recently, the government was showing concern that the number of women in my generation so exceeded the number of men. The economic impact of a coming generation that would be so much smaller than the previous one was alarming. More alarming for Danielle, Simone and Honorine was the prospect of never marrying for sheer lack of members of the male sex.

"It's been fun," Honorine said, teasing Luc. "He's not bad, and it's better than being one of the old maids."

Simone's grip tightened on my arm and I was suddenly as terrified as I had been in the trenches. I reached for my glass, affected and laugh and prayed my bowels didn't turn to water.

Luc spoke about his new job, the increase in salary and getting used to sleeping in a bed that didn't move again. He was happy and content with the prospect of a new life. Honorine seemed a suitable girl for him, admiring his strength of character, recognising his vulnerabilities and feeling his affection. You could see the vision of their life together in her eyes and it was affecting.

"Remember Ilya?" Luc asked, mercifully diverting me. "One of his Russian friends persuaded him to go work for the ballet. He's set-building for some new production that supposed to be another earthquake."

"Ballet Russes?"

"Probably. I don't know about these things," he said, turning to kiss Honorine.

We moved to less expensive drink, and continued our stories and laughter until it was dark and the evening crowd had moved in.

"Would you like some supper?" I asked. "The food isn't bad here, or one of my usual haunts is across the street."

For a moment, it looked like Simone was the only one to like the idea, but Honorine glanced at Luc then nodded enthusiastically.

We moved down the road to the Flamel and

continued our lively chatter. I became aware of Simone looking at me and imagined she was calculating a move.

As the plates were being cleared and the last of the wine poured, I looked at my watch, stood up suddenly and put a handful of notes on the table.

"An engagement present, Luc," I said, shook his hand, said good-night to Honorine and Simone and moved swiftly to the door.

My escape would have been a complete success had I not walked straight into Natasha, who through surprise or affection, hugged me.

XX
Pianoforte

I didn't look back to see the reaction; dealing with that would have to wait for another day. I moved Natasha out the doorway quickly and onto the pavement. Although I was pushing and pulling her unceremoniously, she did not protest and after the first few steps trotted alongside as I strode down the street, even taking my arm.

We went into another café and I found a table about halfway back from the window. I asked Natasha if she wanted anything to eat, but she just asked for a glass of wine.

Neither of us said anything while we waited for the wine. She continued to look healthy, and was dressed more modishly than she usually did, though her dress was several years old, and her coat even older.

"Mme Goncharova has us working hard. At least now when it rains I can afford to take a bus," she said, nervously. "We've been working on new ballet costumes but there have been terrible fights with Mme Nijinska, Diaghilev and Madame – I'm sorry, did I interrupt something important?"

Her words came out jerkily and in a rush, not her

usual, carefully phrased and modulated sentences.

"I can see now that it was not a convenient time - "

She was about to go on when I stopped her, with the help of the waiter who put glasses and a bottle before us.

"We haven't seen you in a long time, Natasha. How have you been?" I asked, pouring her a glass. "Would you like some bread?"

I didn't wait for an answer but signalled the waiter, while Natasha drank half her glass. I filled it again. She looked at it but didn't drink.

I waited for her to speak.

The waiter placed a basket of bread on the table and Natasha shifted her gaze to it.

"Your playing the last time I saw you was wonderful," I said.

"The duchess is the real pianist," she said, her face betraying no satisfaction in the compliment.

"Duchess?"

"Princess," she corrected herself. "She and André have not been married long. For many years, people expected them to marry, but André was at sea, and Anya in the country."

"Did they marry in Paris?"

"In 1918."

After the Revolution.

"Are you still living with the students?"

Natasha laughed.

"Oh, yes," she laughed. "Their work, their drinking, their love affairs and ambitions are refreshing. They are so *passionate* about everything. It's wonderful to be near them."

"It sounds like work is exciting, too," I said.

She frowned and shook her head.

"The arguments there are different. They are not about the passion for the idea, they're about the passion for their egos. They are pointless arguments, and destructive in the way student arguments never are. We do one thing, then after half a morning of noise and arguments, we do something else."

She sounded disillusioned.

"The ballet will be exciting regardless of the costumes," she said. "Everyone is talking about it."

Everyone except the people I knew.

"What is it?"

"*Les Noces*. Stravinsky again, and everyone is saying it is as important as *Le Sacre du Printemps*. You and Danielle should come," she said with animation, then stopped.

"Oh!" she said, looking straight at me. "Is that what I interrupted?"

"*No, it's not.*"

She regarded me for a moment, then continued.

"It's on in June, but before that, Koussevitzky is back.

Two piano concerts. Come to both."

She spoke for the next twenty minutes about pianists and music I'd never heard of with great enthusiasm. Briefly, she looked young and untroubled as she talked of touch, phrasing, chromatic progressions, and dynamic resonances. It was wonderful to see her delight, yet I was feeling quite stupid for barely understanding any of what she said.

When she finished, I noticed that during her descriptions of the music of Bach, Mozart, Chopin, Liszt and Debussy, she had managed to eat all the bread and drink most of the wine.

My description of the encounter the next week caused Danielle to laugh in a more relaxed way than I'd seen of late.

"Don't worry about feeling stupid, either," she added. "I doubt Natasha knows much about grain grinding or the classifications of powder fineness."

We agreed that we should attend both concerts and planned to go to the theatre for tickets on the weekend.

"We can also go to the galleries," she suggested.

We hadn't been back to Rue la Boëtie since the first visit, and I wanted to look in at Galerie Hébrard again.

છ

"So much of what I see and hear, I don't like," Danielle confessed over an after-work glass of wine later in the week. "I want to see and hear what's going on, but to me, it is all so confused. I don't recognise shapes or sounds, and I don't know whether they are worth spending time thinking about. The events are fun, though."

Two years ago, Danielle would never have admitted such insecurity about such things, at least, not to me. This was yet another change in her manner that I noticed after my chance encounter with Luc and Simone, but I didn't see how it could be related to that since I hadn't mentioned it to her.

Describing the change is, even now, very difficult, because Danielle was always confident; confident about herself and her place in the business. She was certainly confident about her ability to do her job. When she was with me, she retained much of that confidence, but appeared willing to surrender it; to defer to my decisions, tastes and whims. She did this, somehow, without being clingy, fawning, silly, or any of those other things that young women do to ingratiate themselves with their men. Though I now appreciated their desperation, as a tactic, I found it unattractive and cloying.

Danielle appeared to be moving beyond this, and it wasn't that she demonstrated less affection for me, but it had a self-reliant strength about it that had not been there before.

"I agree with you completely," I said. "This is our new

city, we should know what's going on, but to me, it is growing in incomprehensibility, not creating the unity that one should hope for."

"Shouldn't art and music bring people together?" she asked.

"Well, not drive them apart. What would your parents have made of *Les Mariés de la Tour Eiffel*?"

"They would have hated every minute," she laughed.

"That's what makes me suspect the whole business," I said. "It makes me more convinced that it's all a big lie."

"What's a lie?"

"Everyone is behaving like there will be no more wars. That's what we've been told, but it isn't true; I'm sorry, but it just isn't," I said.

I could see that the thought was upsetting Danielle, but didn't stop.

"That delusion is making people think that what they do has no consequences; that they can do anything," I continued.

"I hate it when you talk like this," she said, but not crossly.

"I hate it, too, Danielle. More than you can know; but look around. Nothing has changed, not even in our tiny lives: prices go up, suppliers are late; customers complain – that's no different than it was a hundred years ago," I said, trying not to rant. "That's why holding to some old values is so important; we cannot be certain of the worth of the new ones.

"Think of the pictures we've seen, or the music we've heard, or the stories we've read: some we like, others we don't, but are you ready to discard everything we liked before? Of course not, but there are those who are; those who espouse the revolutionary spirit, who would tear the world down to replace it with their version of some grand vision."

When I stopped, I looked at Danielle who looked serene, and it surprised me.

"You'll feel better after you've had something to eat," she said. "Come along."

XXI
En Route

It wasn't until the first weekend in April that we went to buy our tickets for the two concerts. We then continued on, first to Galerie Hébrard, then to the Rosenberg Galerie.

The most notable piece at Galerie Hébrard was a Degas bronze of a young ballerina. What was remarkable was that it was dressed in a real tutu, giving the impression that it was some modernist assembly rather than a traditional bronze.

There were other good pieces along with some odd shapes by French and Italian sculptors. There was also a large gloomy piece of a kneeling woman by the same artist who had created the bust of Natasha.

"The new things were interesting but most of it was rather dead," Danielle said as we walked out into the sunlight. "I'm not sure what the brightly polished pieces were supposed to be, but I thought they were elegant."

I shared Danielle's disappointment. To revive our spirits, we stopped for an ice cream and sat in the sun. Serendipitous stops for glacés were not typical of what we did, but Danielle's new ease encouraged me to suggest such things, and she was usually agreeable.

Work was going well. The company continued to prosper and had reached its new stable size. Changes in the tax regime and import and export regulations varied, but that was normal in commerce, and ways to resolve such difficulties could be found with patience and imagination.

We watched the crowds stream by. Danielle would make an occasional comment about someone's fashion sense, but for much of the time closed her eyes and faced the sun.

"Where do you think you'll be ten years from now?" she asked, not turning from the sun.

I didn't reply.

"Do you not wonder sometimes?" she prompted.

"No."

"I wonder about it every day. I wonder how much longer I will live with my parents; how many years I will buy and sell grains; what there will be to show for it."

She sounded curious rather than bitter.

"Are you discontented?" I asked.

She laughed as she took the last spoonful of ice cream.

"No, I'm not," she said easily. "Perhaps I should be. I am remarkably content to watch what is going on around me, as I think you said you were."

"That's not quite what I said. I think there is a difference between contentment and complacency," I said. "For example, I'd like to think that I am getting better at my job; that a year from now I might have a little more money saved; that my apartment might be a little more comfortably furnished; that I could afford to have a very good meal more often."

"Are you asking for a pay rise?"

I laughed.

"You know what I mean; those are essentially the questions you just said you were asking."

I put some change on the table and we walked towards Rue la Boëtie. When I caught up with Danielle, she easily put her hand on my arm and resumed the conversation.

"I suppose life is about doing the same thing day after day," she said. "The trick is to enjoy what you're doing and not flit about hoping to find something better."

"Do you like what you do?" I asked. "Or do you feel trapped?"

She didn't change her pace, but she was quiet for some time.

"I *do* like what I do," she said eventually. "I try not to ask myself that too often, but it's a question that needs to be asked – *and answered* – a few times each year.

"I don't feel trapped, but often wonder if I would – *could* – have got my job if it wasn't my father's business."

I burst out laughing.

That made her stop. For a moment, I thought she was going to strike me, but she retained her thoughtful, calm demeanour.

"Would you like to explain?"

We moved to the edge of the pavement, under a tree.

"All right. I have no doubt that you *could* have got the job you have. You have the ability, and your father is someone who is capable of recognising talent.

"Whether you would have *wanted* that job had there been no family connection is another question all together," I said, and prepared to duck.

Danielle appeared unfazed by the comment.

"I don't think it would have ever occurred to me to apply for a job there," she said after considering it. "What girl knows anything about industrial processes? Only after failing to get jobs on the favourite list would one start looking at the more general ads."

"What would you have looked for? Did you ever consider that?"

"Of course I did!" Danielle laughed. "I wasn't born with a disposition to grain dealing.

"I think something in fashion, theatre, art, magazine work, maybe something in the wine trade, like your friends – it would have had to be something clerical, I had no artistic, design or sewing talent, or any special abilities, though I did well enough at school," she said. "Further down the list were the duller commercial jobs: banking, insurance, shipping, transportation."

She laughed again.

"It's so unglamorous; so unambitious."

"It's all right to have a dull job that pays the bills as long as your life outside work makes it worth it," I said.

She didn't reply, and I knew I had caused her to think of Henri, her dead fiancé.

"It's better than it was," she said, and began to walk on.

We passed a large building that was undergoing a major renovation, though from what to what wasn't clear, though even on Saturday the work was carrying on.

"What about you, Charles?" Danielle asked. "What would you have done had the war not intervened?"

It was a good question. I had not fully decided.

Montmirail was wine country and my father bought oak for making casks. It was a job I could respect because I could see how it fit into a process. Explaining grain powder to a child would be much harder, though even as a schoolboy, I did not see my future in buying oak or making barrels.

"I barely got to the stage when I thought about it," I said. "The war began just as boys were having those conversations and I never had the chance to think it through.

"Once at the front, the only plan was to wake up the next morning."

I needed to say more, otherwise Danielle would be sad all day.

"I'd shown some promise in mechanical drawing," I continued. "So, I had been thinking of being a draftsman of some sort. By the end of the war, I was at the age when I should have had the skill and some experience but didn't."

"Didn't you dream about being famous or heroic? Achieving great things?"

"Every day I saw what happened to men who tried to achieve great things."

She moved her hand from my arm and took my hand and squeezed it.

"I can tell you one thing," I said, briefly turning to look at her. "I'm perfectly content working where I am."

She nodded.

"But not complacent, I hope."

XXII
Wet Paint

Although we had not been to the gallery for some months, the assistant recognised and greeted us, though not by name. There were about a dozen people looking around and chatting, some loudly. I did a quick mental count and counted at least six different languages being spoken by the visitors.

The proprietor was with a German couple talking about a recently acquired piece by Hervé, as I was later told by the assistant when he reported a successful sale.

Danielle was drawn to a Léger whose work we had seen before. Danielle had described it as being "modern without being threatening."

I was about to join her when the door opened again and Vladimir Orloff and Murphy, the American we had met, came in. The proprietor saw him and nodded, but returned to the Germans who looked interested in adding to their collection.

"Ah, Natasha's friends," Orloff said, stepping towards us.

Murphy had drifted away after giving us a nod and was looking at pictures.

Danielle joined me, and we reminded Orloff of our names.

"Natasha told me of some turmoil at the ballet," I said.

Orloff shook his head.

"It's been as bad as anything I've seen," he said with a dramatic flourish. "Bronislava and Sergei are about to throw out Natalia's costumes and sets, which will mean remaking everything in six weeks. Gerald!"

The American came over.

"You remember Natasha's friends from the concert," Orloff said.

Gerald smiled and shook our hands.

"They have heard about the impending disaster," Orloff said.

"Mme Goncharova has issued a distress call and needs people to help repaint the sets and help with costumes. Why don't you join us next Saturday," Gerald said.

"And Sunday, and Monday, and Tuesday," Orloff added to underline the urgency and the amount of work to be done. "A dancer can't just put on a costume the day before the performance; it has to be practised in so that it moves correctly and is seen properly in the lights. Natasha will let you know when and where to go."

I was about to say that seeing Natasha was no sure thing, but the proprietor had finished with the Germans and came to greet Vladimir and Gerald.

We walked around the gallery and liked much of what we saw. Some names were by now familiar, but there were new ones, rich with colour, form and life.

"Do you really want to paint sets?" Danielle asked, wholly unconvinced of my enthusiasm.

"It's one day," I said. "It might be fun. We'll be able to say we once did theatre work."

"*We'll* be able to say?" she challenged.

"We might meet Sergei, Bronislava, Natalia and maybe even Igor," I teased, exaggerating the first-name familiarity.

Danielle laughed loudly enough that heads turned to ensure we weren't mocking the artwork.

"It will depend whether Natasha gets in touch with us or not," I said. "Given that I've just seen her, I wouldn't expect to see her before May."

೮

Not for the first time, Natasha surprised us and made contact with Danielle on Wednesday. She approached her on her way home and spoke to her only long enough to give a time, place and tell her that she really hoped to see us there.

What we should have foreseen was that when we got there, everyone was speaking Russian. We were unceremoniously given paint brushes and directed to different locations within the factory-like rehearsal rooms.

Danielle was sent to work on costumes, while I found myself with a collection of men that might have been found on an American chain gang. (That was Gerald's observation.) We found ourselves working near each other, and he chatted in French to me as Russians shouted at each other around us.

There was a sailing ship quantity of canvas to be painted. Many flats had eight or ten coats of paint on them already, while others were frames that needed to have material stretched over them, then tacked and painted.

Amid the noise, Diaghilev appeared, impeccably dressed and wandered without fear through the groups of painters. He greeted many by name, and ignored others, like me. As he reached the end of the room a woman started screaming at him in Russian. He declined to reply in kind but said a few words in a normal voice which only infuriated her further. He then turned to one of the workers who relayed an instruction to clear an area around the piano. Flats that had been on the floor being fitted with canvas were raised and manoeuvred to the edge of the room, while others were moved away from the windows to let the light in.

Presently, four dancers in stylised costumes in subdued tones came in. Two of them were looking at their hands which had paint on them, while the other two walked with their hands in the air.

A man in a suit with moustache and glasses came in and went to the piano. After a few words with the dancers, he began to play and the dancers began their extraordinary movements. Bronislava Nijinska appeared near the piano and scrutinised the dancers.

She shouted something in Russian and everyone stopped while she went up to one of the dancers and adjusted the costume, getting paint on her hands in the process. She called for a seamstress to pin a renegade fold on each of the dancers, then they tried the movement again. She stopped them again and approached a dancer and changed the position of the pin.

The music started again with the one ballerina dancing. Mme Nijinska nodded and the seamstress made the adjustments on the others. They started the dance again and it went for a minute until she had a word with the pianist who stopped and they all left the room.

We got back to work, but there were similar interruptions until about six in the evening when I went to find Danielle.

She and Natasha had been painting effects on the costumes. Up close, they looked roughly made and finished, but the impression they had made on the dancers in motion was one of carefully created detail.

"Was it dreadful?" I asked Danielle as we walked

home. "You must be tired."

"I'm all right," she said. "I expect to be stiff in the morning, but Natasha looked exhausted. She's been doing this all week."

"Were you able to talk to her?" I asked, and explained how Gerald had been good enough to speak French to me.

"Gerald's wife, Sara, was there, too. She was good company and worked without complaining. Natasha translated some of the Russian tantrums for us. That was funny, too."

"So, are we going to see whatever it is?" I asked.

"It's called *Les Noces*."

XXIII

Concerts, Costumes & Cacophony

One of the trickiest things in setting down these recollections is separating the memories of the time
from those seen through the lens of history. I never did
anything truly artistic in my life, but now when conversation turns to discussions of music or theatre, I can say
that I once painted sets for the Ballet Russes.

Maybe it's age, but the open, spontaneity seems to
have gone out of such things. Modern productions may
have their moments of drama, even disorder, but no
longer is there the near chaos of creativity amid an army
of volunteer amateurs trying to get a piece ready for performance on time.

We saw many people who were or would become famous in those weeks, but such encounters were a
miniscule part of my life which has been blessedly mundane.

There were five events in May and June, each of which
would have been remarkable, but Danielle and I felt *trop
d'une bonne chose*, and once they were over, we retreated
back to our invisible lives.

It was hard not to let the two piano concerts blur into

each other, not because they were not distinctive, but because our knowledge of the repertory made identifying what we heard difficult to remember; you can only remember things with language, even if it's metaphor.

What I can remember is Wanda Landowska playing the harpsichord, an instrument I had only heard once or twice before, and filling the vast auditorium with precise sound. Similarly, the young Casadesus seemed to make each note ring, playing with dexterity and passion – characteristics that I could identify and appreciate.

We also heard a symphony by Prokofiev, who was there to hear it. Unlike other music of his we had heard, this little symphony was either in homage or parody of Handel and Mozart. The audience's reactions split into three, aligned to the different levels of the theatre: those in the orchestra, *baignoires*, and *premiere loges*, tutted; those in the *dieuxieme* and *troisieme loges*, laughed in recognition of what they saw as the joke, while those in the amphitheatre and *cinquieme* cheered uncritically.

Danielle and I, seated in *troisieme loges*, were amused, but uncertain whether we should be.

We saw Natasha after both concerts, but no one else familiar, the Russians apparently not thinking enough of Prokofiev to turn out in force. We bought a glass of wine for Natasha, but she seem drunk on the music and chattered about it until Danielle and I had finished our drink and were tempted to drink hers. We did see "Mademoiselle" at both concerts but she went back stage to talk to the soloists instead of joining us for drinks.

❦

One event of cultural note that did not involve Natasha was our visit to the exhibition of the Salon des Indépendants at the Grand Palais. Vladimir Orloff had told us that Gerald would be submitting a piece, and having seen him spread brown paint on the sets for *Les Noces*, we thought it would be fun to go; he was the only artist we had knowingly met.

The crowds in the allocated space at the Grand Palais made navigating the rooms difficult, and crowds before individual pictures stopped the already slow flow of traffic. Following a curious arrangement that placed paintings in alphabetical order by artist so as to ensure *égalité*, we waded through half the exhibition to see the one picture we came to see.

It was called *Razor*, and, I thought, held its place well. It was almost a metre square, and had strong, clean lines and used what I heard called "a muted pallet" of "flat colours". Danielle thought it made sense; I was busy being amused by the three objects featured: a box of matches, a red fountain pen and what the Americans call a "safety razor." The razor and pen were crossed. I found the sharp edges and flat colours very pleasing; orderly, balanced, and somehow satisfying. What, if anything, it meant, I had no idea.

I turned to look for Danielle and felt myself being pushed along by the crowd as it pressed on to the next sensation. I looked for her while trying not to trample the people ahead of me, and saw her in a quiet pool talking to a friend as the mob swirled about them.

I signalled that I'd meet her outside, for although there were allegedly masterpieces everywhere, the combination of the crowds, noise, stuffiness and inability to actually look at anything before being caught up in the current of impatient art lovers, I had had enough.

I went out and found a bench in the gardens that bordered Avenue Alexandre III and enjoyed the warmth of the sun. Danielle took her time, as I hoped she would, and joined me half an hour later. She attributed these occasional escapes from crowds as being related to my war experiences; I put them down to boredom and impatience.

She, too, appeared to be relieved by the sunlight and fresh air and sat with me, idly talking, for another half hour.

"Who was your friend?" I asked. "She looked familiar."

"Oh, Charles, it was, Sara! You met her on the painting day," she chided. "She's very proud of Gerald. He's never really painted before and now spends much of his time working on his pictures."

"I thought it was very good."

"So did I," Danielle agreed. "I told her so; she only said that she hoped someone would buy it as she didn't have room for it in their apartment."

℘

The performance of *Les Noces* was the culmination of eager anticipation, rumours of something revolutionary, and of hot-tempered artistic disputes.

After seeing it – all twenty-five minutes of it – I was not alone in feeling greatly let down. The audience's reaction was split to say the least. The music proceeded in a chant like manner with little variation of volume or tempo, and indeed, to me sounded like the endless repetition of something not worth hearing the first time.

Danielle was bitterly disappointed that in the event, the costumes she had worked on were not used and everyone was dressed in brown and white – making for possibly the dreariest wedding of the century. The men's costumes had at least a slight feel of the rustic about them with cross-gartered stockings and brown trousers – more like pantaloons; but the women's dowdy tunics were, as I heard one person remark, "like those worn at less good British boarding schools." To which his companion replied, "They may have been."

"I wonder what Natasha made of all that," Danielle

said as we walked for a much-needed drink at *L'Homme d'Affaires*. "It was so – *joyless*."

ɞ

Natasha thought it was wonderful.

By the time we saw her, two day's later at a café after work, the enthusiastic reviews had been read by many and the ballet was, apparently, the talk of *tout le monde*. I don't think our reticence to join in the adulation was welcomed by Natasha, but she smiled.

"Well, if you can keep what you think to yourselves, there is a special party on Sunday – on a barge. *Everyone* is going to be there. Come to the Quai d'Orsay just before seven, near the Chamber of Deputies," she said quickly. "Vladimir and Gerald said you could come since you helped with the scenery and costumes."

"Not that there was much," I muttered to Danielle, who smacked my arm lightly and tried to stifle a laugh.

Later when Danielle and I were at the office, I could tell by the way she studiously avoided my eyes that something was wrong.

"I wasn't going to lie to her," I said, guessing what was at the root of the problem.

She put her pen down and looked at me. I was expecting to get the sort of dressing down that new clerks and inaccurate accountants received. When she said nothing, I began to feel that I may have been wrong.

Just when I was about to speak, she did:

"You're right. It was grim."

Our laughter attracted glances from the hallway as people passed, but Danielle didn't care.

"Does that mean you don't want to go to the party?" I asked.

"Of course it doesn't! Meet me at the entrance to Gare d'Orsay at six-thirty."

From Natasha's Diary

1923

I have survived another year, but it is not getting easier as I had hoped. There is more suspicion; more worry, and the daemons are becoming stronger, attracting support from around the world.

Mademoiselle continues to be gracious and generous but is not pleased with my playing this summer and is making me practice more. I continue to help Sandra cook, and her mother still tells her that everything she does is wrong, but doesn't lift a finger to help. I feel sorry for Sandra, but she simply laughs and continues to prepare meal after meal.

There is much talk here about the concerts by Mme Landowska and Casadesus. Endless arguments about whose interpretation was better, and who relied more on technique. The other night there was a discussion about Les Noces. *Apparently Charles and Danielle were not the only ones not to like it.*

A student I had come to know revealed that I had worked on the costumes and was at the performance, so I was pressed for an opinion.

I was able to divert their attention by telling about the party on the barge and all the people who were there.

They thought the idea of dozens of toys piled up for table decorations was very funny. Along with Diaghilev, Mme Goncharova was there (reading palms), but interestingly, not Mme Nijinksa. Ansermet, who had conducted was there, of course, along with Germaine Taillefer and Milhaud, and the American songwriter, Cole Porter. There was also Jean Cocteau – who is afraid of water; getting him on the barge was a problem – and Tristan Tzara, the great poseur.

I had started by talking to two people but by the time I was telling about how Boris Kochno and Ansermet held the giant wreath with Les Noces *written on it and Stravinsky jumping through it, the whole table was silent.*

One wonders what they'd think if I mentioned someone really important.

XXIV

Les Noces II

1923-1924

Christmas was very different this year. I spent it with Danielle and her family for the first time. They had asked me before, but this year there was a good reason to accept: Danielle and I announced our engagement. We'd agreed to get married in early November, but Danielle wanted to enjoy the secret for a while, and carefully think about it before making it public.

For more than three years we'd been moving closer, but neither of us was ready to open ourselves to the level of trust to allow love to germinate. Once we admitted the possibility, there were endless discussions about working together, never being able to escape business, and how we really felt about each other.

Neither of us was deluded into expecting – or demanding – the breathless excitement of first love; we'd both suffered too much for that; but, little by little, we let our defences down, and it was an odd feeling. Danielle admitted that she felt more fear than any other emotion but the confident calm I had detected the previous spring continued to assert itself.

As the fresh leaves of 1924 began to unfold, our

romantic feelings were given a push by Luc and Honorine's wedding. Danielle pronounced it the happiest wedding she'd ever been to. Their happiness engulfed both sets of parents, other family members and friends. Even Luc's sister, Simone, appeared thoroughly happy – enough that she welcomed both Danielle and me as if we were family.

Later, I saw the reason for her happiness: she had found herself a young man and clearly had plans for her wedding to follow her brother's soon. Having had a taste of her determination, I could see there was no escape for this new fellow. He was a lucky man, as Simone was vivacious, fun and not afraid of hard work. I could see those things the previous Christmas, but was unable to respond. I now suspected that it was because my feelings for Danielle had already begun to evolve.

Danielle's parents were delighted with our decision, and the rest of the office simply noted that it was about time. Danielle herself while openly more affectionate, remained remarkably unaffected by our new condition.

We had no immediate plans to marry, thinking that earlier in the following year would give us the chance to get used to the idea and find a place to live. The wedding itself would be simple; we both had parents, but no siblings and few cousins. Nevertheless, these plans pushed other activities down our list of priorities.

Art and music didn't receive the attention it previously had. In October, we went to see *Within the Quota*, which Gerald had written with Cole Porter. The music was a welcome change from both the heavy, serious music and the incomprehensible which had become our regular diet. Hearing lively, jazzy tunes at a ballet was thoroughly refreshing and engendered feelings of hope and well-being.

As with many events and people we saw, we thought they were good and entertaining but were wholly unaware of their wider significance. That this cheerful ballet would come to be recognised as the first real American ballet never occurred to us.

Natasha saw us there but didn't have time to chat as she was rushing off to Mme Duflot's – along with a good number of the audience, she said. She did ask us to meet her the next day at a café in Montparnasse.

When she met us, she had come from a visit to Prince André and Princess Anya and was upset when she arrived. Danielle and I had glasses of wine, but Natasha ordered tea, into which she stirred strawberry jam, provided by a waiter who was obviously familiar with her and other Russians in the neighbourhood.

"Believe it or not, you are among my closest friends," she began urgently. "I can say that you are my best French friends – artists and lovers don't count. There are things

I want to tell you, but with them are things that are dangerous to know."

She drank half a cup of her tea which appeared to still be at an alarming temperature.

"Prince André has just told me that he is leaving France, and I am heart-broken," she said, her voice catching. "He will go first to England where the company has an office and he can continue to work. If England becomes unsafe, he will try to go to America."

"Why should he not be safe?" Danielle asked. "This is Paris."

"It is to do with being Russian," she said.

"There are all sorts of people here," Danielle said, sounding affronted at the implication that the city was anything but open and tolerant, if not welcoming.

Natasha sighed and began to explain.

"There are Russians and there are Russians. While many of the aristocracy who escaped are here, there are the lower classes, too, like many at the ballet and opera. The former aristocrats are disguising themselves as business men, or ordinary workers," she said.

I remembered the story that Ilya who worked on the wine barges was allegedly one of them.

She finished her tea and waved for another cup.

"What we have now in Paris are a number of aristocrats pretending to be bourgeois, and a growing number of the proletariat pretending to be aristocrats."

Danielle giggled indicating where such things figured among the concerns of the world. She quickly stopped herself and actually blushed.

"Don't worry," Natasha said with a slight smile. "To the rest of the world it is of no matter, but those of us who harbour thoughts of regaining power, seeking revenge, or simply clinging to memories, the evidence of who we really are is very important.

"Unfortunately, it is especially important to those who can profit from it," she continued. "So, in a futile attempt to separate the sheep from the goats, André tells me that there is to be a Commission for Nobility which will supposedly 'authenticate' all claimants to titles."

"Why does Prince André object?" Danielle asked.

Natasha drank a good part of her new tea, then added more jam. She shook her head sadly.

"Because he is an honourable man. He doesn't have to prove anything to anyone, and neither does Anya. Together they owned hundreds of thousands of acres, including several small cities. He was a distinguished naval officer. Who has the authority to judge *his* standing?

"He wants no part of it. He also has no respect for Kirill Vladimirovich who is the man behind the commission."

"The man who might have been at the concert?" I said. "Yes."

"There are others who are on the edges of things like Vladimir whose father's connection with the dowager duchess could place him in danger from all sides, should there be violence."

"Violence is unlikely, isn't it?" I asked, remembering what Danielle had said.

"Oh, it's very likely," Natasha said. "It's tribal war, and it's already started."

XXV
Preparations

1924

We saw no signs of Natasha's predicted disorder; our lives cruised along smoothly with its normal rhythms of business, the seasons and the odd night at the opera, a concert or exhibition. Occasionally, we went to the race track with Danielle's parents who were fond of going to the races, though they knew nothing about horses, didn't ride and seldom wagered more than a few francs. What they liked was the colour, the noise, the excitement and watching races with friends and a good claret.

We braved the Grand Palais again to see the *Indépendants*. Gerald had two pictures on show, including an enormous canvas of part of a ship that was at least five metres tall and more than four wide. Its size had the effect of making the other pictures on the wall look ridiculous. With the ballet and his paintings, he had made his mark on Paris and, according to Vladimir, was ready to move to Antibes.

I was going to ask Vladimir about what Natasha had said, but Danielle stopped me, saying it was neither the time nor the place to ask such questions.

"Besides, we don't know how he fits into things," she said once we were outside.

"Don't we?" I asked. "He's Diaghilev's cousin and his father was the dowager duchess's banker. Natasha's known him for years."

She wasn't convinced.

"I don't like any of it, and if I didn't think Natasha somehow relied on us, I would seriously consider losing touch with her," she said vehemently.

"As if it would be up to us," I said. "Besides, if Vladimir is leaving, and André and Anya, her circle of friends will be contracting."

"Just like a garrotte."

⁒

We set a date for our wedding. We'd have it in February 1925. We thought it would help everyone through the winter and hasten the spring. I had found an apartment that Danielle instantly liked. It was in the same building as my flat and was immediately below it, though it was larger. Danielle liked that I knew the building and the neighbourhood.

Having only lived at home, Danielle's concerns about finding a place to live were new to her, and her natural naivety about the whole concept amused me. On this matter, her normal confidence gave way to teenaged anxiety, and she was relieved to have it resolved.

We would take possession in January, and I would move in and be able to keep an eye on the renovations and decoration. There was not a lot to do, but the bureaucratic business had to be taken care of; Danielle's command of the situation returned and I knew things had to be done properly.

☙

When August came, Danielle and her family headed for Les Sables de d'Olonne while I headed for what I hoped would be a quiet guest house in Deauville.

When the French holidays begin, tens of thousands of people attempt to escape Paris, and many of them appeared to be on my train. It was a very long train, I was in a compartment with one other gentleman who appeared to want the same as I did: quiet to think and read.

The journey was sublimely leisurely with neither of us saying anything, but engrossed in watching the scenery, or our reading. I was reading *La Prisonnière*, the fifth or sixth volume of Proust, depending how you counted.

There was a pleasant restaurant car, and so it was that in a state of deep contentment, I read and dozed, ate and drank, rattled and rolled the hours away to Deauville. On arrival, even before the steam and smoke cleared from the platform, the smell of the sea proved that Paris was far behind.

I took a taxi to my guest house which was really an

hotel with a wish to retain traditional customs and stand-ards. It did this with varying success. It was comfortable, well maintained, and friendly without being intrusive.

My room did not face the sea, but I could hear it and smell it, and that was enough. I had reckoned that if I were only in my room to sleep, then it wouldn't matter if I couldn't see the sea as long as I could hear it.

Though not large, the room was comfortable and had a desk and chair I could sit and read in, if the weather were inclement. I could imagine Proust writing about a hundred-fifty pages about such a room, but I shall leave it here.

A large number of guests had been coming here for years and the hotel's continuing eccentricities resulted from that inertia.

For example, there were usually two choices of meal for dinner, except on Saturday evening and Sunday lunch. Bottles of wine only partially drunk would be retained and placed on your table the next day. All alcoholic drinks consumed in the dining room had to be paid for – in cash – at the end of the meal, but the comfortable bar that opened onto the lush garden would keep an account of your drinks and present you with a bill at the end of your stay. Everything was recorded by your name; never your room number.

While many newspapers could be found in the foyer,

copies could be ordered and claimed at the office. There was no reception desk. The average age of the guests was about three decades older than I, but most were friendly and some characters were very amusing.

By the end of the weekend, I had relaxed enough not to feel guilty about nodding off over my book while reading on the porch after lunch. The food was good, and combined with walks along the beach in the morning, the afternoon and after dinner, I was not only feeling happily relaxed but also well-fed.

That was until Tuesday when, while reading a copy of Monday's *Le Journal*, my stomach turned when I came across an article with the headline:

Grand Duke Kirill Vladimirovich declares himself
Emperor of All the Russias.

From *Natasha's Journal* Diary

1924

I wish I wasn't always right about things.

While I was stunned by Kirill's audacity, I had been expecting it. It is the great Russian characteristic: expect the worst, and still be surprised by it.

The engagement of Charles and Danielle is another matter. It is something I have hoped for almost since I first saw them together, but I did not expect they'd find the courage. Their experiences have damaged them almost as much as mine have damaged me. At least their experiences do not endanger them.

Sandra is not yet married, and Mme Mercier is becoming impatient and goes on with embarrassing talk of grandchildren. Poor Sandra is mortified that such things are discussed in public. She is very happy, and her cooking has improved immeasurably.

Mademoiselle continues to be kind and demanding. Kind in my living and working conditions, but trenchant in her expectations. Yesterday, she made me play the opening fifteen bars of the Beethoven Sonata No. 14 seventeen times, critiquing each rendition. We never got any further. I had thought it was a piece I could play, but Mademoiselle obviously thought not.

I cried for twenty minutes when I got back to my room, but it was mostly for the sheer joy and beauty of finally getting it the way she wanted me to play it. The reality, of course, was that she got me to play it the way I wanted to play it, and even I could hear that I had never played it better.

I cannot deny that I am becoming worried about what will become of me. Old friends are leaving, the departure of André and Anya is a great blow, and Kirill's growing invisible power over the émigrés seems to be pushing me into a corner, or out of Paris. Still, I am not visible in the way that others are.

Poor Danielle and Charles, they would love me to find someone and live a normal life. I am getting closer to telling them why I cannot. Perhaps after they are married.

XXVI
Musings

1924

D anielle described her holiday with her parents as "restful but dull." While gratified that she missed me, I was still getting used to the emotional closeness that Danielle expected, though she was patient.

Natasha had been in Gargenville again in August. When she returned, she appeared refreshed and was more forthcoming about her piano playing than usual. Her lessons had gone well, and she had spent much of the time learning a piece that she wanted to share with us. As she had never done this before, we hoped we'd have the opportunity to hear her play.

One Saturday in late September, she found us at the Flamel. I had introduced Danielle to it when we'd become engaged. Later, when she viewed the potential new flat, one of the reasons she approved was because the Flamel was close by.

Natasha joined us in time to order a meal. Danielle would tease me about my hobby being feeding her.

"Why don't you come to dinner at my parents?" she suggested to Natasha after she had told us about her piano lessons. "It could be any time. Their Pleyel is maintained."

The look on Natasha's face surprised us.

"She looked horrified," Danielle said, after Natasha had left. "But she appeared to be happy at the same time."

"She was bursting with things to tell us, but after you invited her, she – well, she panicked. That's the only way I can say it," I said.

Natasha had managed to decline politely, but said she'd work on a more "convenient" solution.

"I know she's our friend," Danielle began, "but sometimes I wonder if she's quite right."

"You are right," I conceded. "From the first time we met, I wondered about her. I think she has experienced terrible things that she never talks about, at least to us."

Danielle considered this.

"I can't imagine what it must have been like to be caught up in turmoil like that. No doubt she had friends and family killed," she said.

"Did she come here as a refugee? She once told me that she came to Paris as a child, but she has also talked about being fourteen in Saint Petersburg," I said, "She appears to have had a very Russian education, which would have been difficult growing up in Paris. She speaks Russian French, which suggests she hasn't been here that long – unless she was very isolated."

"If she came as a child, that would explain how she

knows so many people," Danielle said. "But how? Where did she make these connections, if not at school? At church? Is she religious?"

I shrugged.

"She must be an aristocrat of some sort," Danielle asserted.

"Unless she's an aristocrat's bastard," I said.

Danielle looked at me and didn't say anything as she thought.

"That makes sense," she began, with a growing feeling of discovery. "Yes; she's provided for, but out of the way. Then, with the revolution, her source of support is killed, displaced, or otherwise cut-off and she's left to fend for herself."

This was like opening the curtains.

"That would be the great upset in her life: she loses her benefactor, and with the loss of money, whoever is looking after her turns her out or is unable to support her," I said.

"How old would she have been in 1917?"

"How old do you think she is now?" I asked.

Danielle considered this, then shook her head.

"Hardship can age people," she said. "She could be as young as twenty, but probably not over twenty-five. I can usually tell by a woman's hands, but hers are so thin, it's hard to tell."

"I met her in early 1921, nearly four years ago," I said. "She was certainly more than sixteen, but how much more. . . .?"

I walked with Danielle halfway back to her parents. It was a ritual. She had said that going all the way there and back to my apartment was too far, besides, she teased, she might have another date waiting at a café nearer home. Natasha remained on her mind as she thought out loud:

"She effortlessly moves through French and Russian social levels and knows all sorts of people," Danielle said. "She appears to exist on very little money; and she never seems to live anywhere for very long. She trusts no one. Not even us. We've known her all that time and don't even know her name."

"Do you suppose she's a ghost?"

Danielle laughed.

"Well, if she is, she's the first one I've heard of with an appetite like that."

❧

Our speculations about Natasha gave way to the practicalities of work. The directors appeared to think that the changed position of Danielle and me should somehow alter our position in the company, as we were duly invited in to discuss it with them. Already there had been the jokes about marrying the boss's daughter, but as most people had been expecting it for a long time, they were without malice.

Nevertheless, when confronted with the reality of patronage, an independent streak I didn't know I had appeared.

During my digression declining the offer or promotion to a directorship *at this time* (I was careful to add), I raised the question about the consequential effects such a move would have. Who would take my job, or Danielle's? What would there be for two of us to do that was not already being done?

What emerged, more through facial expressions than words was that none of them had considered the possibility of Danielle continuing to work.

In truth, I hadn't given it much thought as the shortage of young men to fill positions made it clear to me that for Danielle to continue to work was simple commercial sense, for France had lost more than a million and a half people, soldiers and civilians.

Lest any supposed wisdom be attributed as a result of this analysis, rather significantly, I had failed to discuss this beforehand with Danielle. She accused me of being ungrateful and asked me why I shied from taking on more responsibility.

"It's not the additional work you're afraid of, and you manage people well. Father would love you to take charge one day," she said.

In the silence that followed, she found the answer. She took my arm and put her head on my chest.

"You have taken charge, haven't you?" she asked, not expecting an answer. "It must have been terrible. I will tell Papa. It will not be mentioned again, unless you feel you want to."

The truth was that "taking charge" was an insignificant thing with unspeakable consequences. What it came down to was receiving a piece of paper and shouting "*Allons-y!*" and watching twenty-three of the people you'd just had breakfast with die.

I would take charge of Danielle and my garden, and that would be enough.

XXVII

Toccata

1924

One evening in November, Natasha was waiting for us when we left the office on Rue du Jour. She looked cold and must have been standing there for half an hour.

"You could have come in to the office and waited where it was warm," Danielle said, taking her ungloved hand and rubbing it.

"That would not have been convenient," she replied.

"Well, do it any way," Danielle retorted in her managerial voice.

"Let's get a drink," I said before the exchanges got out of hand.

We went to the *Café L'Homme d'Affaires*, and I ordered a *marc* for Natasha. She tried to order a red wine, as we did, but Danielle was still in charge.

"If you're going to wait in the cold without gloves, scarf or warm overcoat, you'll drink what Charles tells you."

Natasha was quiet as we waited to be served.

Since we'd become engaged, Danielle had been more robust in ensuring that friends didn't take undue advantage of me. I don't think this was from any growing sense of possession, jealousy, or fear that I'd spend money on other people that should be spent on her, but rather that some friends – especially Natasha – unconsciously (or not) assumed I'd look after them. This more often included time and emotional investment than financial outlay, but Danielle said that if I couldn't look after my own interests, she'd have to.

By the time the drinks arrived, Natasha was shaking and Danielle and I whispered that we should get her somewhere near a fire.

When she'd drunk half the glass, grimacing with each sip, her hands steadied and she was breathing more slowly and calmly.

"Can you come with me?" she asked when she felt we'd listen to her.

"Do you need help?" Danielle asked, sounding concerned, and a little chastened.

"No; not really," Natasha said. "André and Anya are expecting us."

She looked embarrassed that she'd given no notice and it was our instinct to decline, but Danielle spoke.

"Of course. It would be lovely to see them."

Natasha smiled for the first time, finished her drink, and glanced a the clock behind the bar.

"We are going to be late," she said.

"We'll get a taxi," Danielle said. "Come along."

She drained her glass, and we left.

A fire burned brightly in the Rostov's apartment and Danielle moved Natasha to it as soon as we'd greeted them.

Danielle explained to Anya why Natasha was so cold and André fetched her a brandy.

"Please stop fussing!" Natasha exclaimed loudly, but it didn't stop Anya who led her to the sofa before the fire and wrapped an Afghan around her.

Only then did I look around the room and saw that it was now nearly bare apart from the chairs, the two pianos and a desk which now doubled as a drinks cabinet. The sound of Natasha's voice echoing must have made me look.

"You really are leaving," Danielle said, noting my survey of the room.

"Natasha has told you of the possibility of local difficulties," the former prince said. "The rest of our things will go at the end of the month. Anya will go to our new home in London. I will join her before Christmas."

The prince and Anya continued the narrative of their move.

"Who cannot regret leaving Paris," Anya said, "but there is much in London."

"Fog and rain," said Natasha, who appeared more

settled and warmer now.

"There is good music and theatre, shops, galleries and museums," Anya said, undaunted.

"And, greater safety," André added.

"I cannot believe that Paris is unsafe," Danielle said with an element of defiance.

"Mlle Doré, it is not Paris that is unsafe," the prince said, "but certain people who have invaded it, abused its hospitality and not respected its openness."

"Oh!" Anya said suddenly. "The happy reason we wanted to see you! Congratulations!"

She moved to Danielle and embraced her and then me. André kissed Danielle's hand and shook mine, holding my arm firmly.

"Natasha told us; we are all very happy for you."

A bottle of champagne was produced, and we moved into the dining room where a small collation of food awaited.

"Forgive us, but we are more limited in what can be prepared here every day," Anya said.

Danielle laughed as she looked at the assortment of sliced ham, smoked salmon, new potatoes, peas with pearl onions, and a salad with grains.

"Ah. Bulgur," I said, helping myself.

"You know bulgur?" André asked, surprised. "And here we were trying to offer you something different."

"Stop, teasing, André!" Anya said. "It's one of his projects."

"What, teasing?"

"You see what it does," Anya said affectionately to her husband and sighed. "You tease people and then they never take anything you do seriously."

"I am sorry, Charles," André said seriously. "The ship I was on spent considerable time in the Middle East, this is around 1900. We ate bulgur and I decided to try growing durum wheat at several of my southern estates."

"Near Rostov-on Don?" Natasha asked.

"Yes, there."

So he was *that* Rostov.

"It did well, but there wasn't a taste for it in Russia and most of it was exported back to the Middle East, so it never made much money. How do you know about it?"

I was about to answer when Danielle interrupted.

"Please don't get him started," she said. "It's on the periphery of our business. Are you taking your pianos to England?"

"I have bought a new one," Anya said. "When I found the apartment on Avery Row, I looked for a piano. It's a Broadwood from one of the large private houses that is being torn down for offices. The instruments here are very good, but have no sentimental value. And I can see that Natasha is itching to play!"

We continued our conversation. Natasha was more animated now and talked about some of her friends, but we gathered that she had little work at the moment.

When we'd finished the champagne and the wine, we moved to the main room.

Anya nodded to Natasha.

"Thank you, Princess," she said with a slight bob, and moved to the piano.

André lifted the lid and turned on another light to illuminate the keyboard.

Natasha warmed up her fingers with some arpeggios, then settled on the bench.

"I'd like to play two pieces. The first is Rachmaninoff's *Prelude in G-minor*, and the second is the Prokofiev *Toccata*."

I had heard the Rachmaninoff prelude before and liked its almost humorous lilt, which, I thought, Natasha captured perfectly. By contrast, the *Toccata* was an explosion of modernity with driving staccato rhythms, virtuosic technical demands and unfamiliar harmonies. I loved it. The passion and obvious satisfaction that playing it gave Natasha contributed to my admiration of the piece.

We applauded. André went to the piano to escort her back to her seat, and she giggled.

"Will you play for us, Princess?" she asked.

Anya began to demur, but André nodded.

"It is our friends's last opportunity to hear you play here," he said gently.

She walked to the piano.

"I will also play two pieces," she said, with the confidence of a seasoned performer. "Chopin's *Etude Opus 25, Number 11*, and another Rachmaninoff prelude, *Opus 32, Number 10*, the B-minor."

Anyone reading this will know that such musical knowledge as I have was recently acquired and very superficial – as is my knowledge of art, literature, history, science, and just about anything else.

As a boy, I knew about sports and hunting, but my studies had been commercial, so I knew balance sheets, annual reports, something about insurance and banking, and my mathematics was sound. I had the usual boy's passing interest in astronomy, geology and mechanical things – especially steam-driven – but my uninquisitive environment didn't foster greater depth of study, or enthusiasm.

However, when the princess played the opening notes of both these pieces, I recognised them at once, and appreciated that sitting in this apartment on a cold November night and hearing what I had heard from both performers was something exceptional.

The ending of the prelude makes me think of *Claire*

de Lune; it suddenly seems to be about to go somewhere new, then stops.

Danielle began to make "going home" moves, but André stopped us.

He had a bottle of brandy and two glasses.

"We really can't – " Danielle began.

"Please. I have to tell you something. Some sad news received just before you arrived," he said gravely.

He poured the brandy and gave each of us a glass.

"I learned today that Oleg Petrovich, Count Viktorov, was found dead this afternoon. He was twenty-nine years old."

He crossed himself, as did the others, then raised his glass.

Danielle and I looked puzzled, then, with tears on her cheeks, Natasha turned to me.

"You knew him as Ilya."

XXVIII
Memory Eternal

1924-1925

I have been to too many funerals in my life but had never been to an Orthodox one. Danielle and I slipped in the back of the cathedral in Rue Daru and watched and listened as the centuries old ritual invoked God, the Blessed Virgin and countless saints to receive or intercede for Ilya.

The darkness of the space; the richness of the images, the luminosity of myriad candles, the waves of incense, and the impossible Russian basses singing harmonies of splendour, were transformative. Such was the cold of the building that must have made every Russian feel at home. It was wholly possible to believe that this was a state between earth and heaven when glimpsing immortality was possible.

We learned about Ilya; his respectable family of modest wealth, in Imperial Russian terms; his distinguished service in the Russian Army; his loyalty to the Tsar, and his flight from St Petersburg to Paris.

We saw Prince André and Princess Anya, who were greeted as their former status warranted. We'd expected to see Natasha with them, or with the Russians from the

Ballet Russes who were there, and were surprised to find her at the back of the cathedral at the end of our row wearing a black lace mantilla over her cloche hat. She was familiar with the liturgy and recited prayers and made the responses with confidence and conviction.

Luc and Honorine were there, too, with M. and Mme Barnard and Simone. We caught up with them afterwards at Brasserie La Lorraine, around the corner.

"Catholic funerals are about forty-five minutes," said Mme Barnard once she had her glass of wine. "Two hours is not what we expected."

"It was beautiful and very moving," Simone said.

Indeed, it was obvious that she had been considerably moved, and no doubt felt the pool of eligible men had been further diminished.

Simone had not seen Danielle since we became engaged. She displayed no sign of resentment and extended her congratulations to her. However, she then turned to me and asked:

"What happened to your little Russian doll?"

That confirmed my fear that Simone had jumped to a conclusion when she saw my meeting with Natasha in the doorway of the Flamel. Her question, of course, was designed to pique Danielle, but she only raised an eyebrow.

"Did you not see her sitting with us in the cathedral?" I asked. "She went to the interment, otherwise you could have met her."

"Who paid for this elaborate funeral?" Luc asked. "The coffin, the choir, the church, the undertakers? Ilya didn't have any money, did he?"

That question remained unanswered until we saw Natasha again, which wasn't until two weeks before we were married.

It was a sunny Saturday and we'd decided to walk through the Tuileries and visit a gallery or two in the Louvre. We were walking down Allée de Diane when she walked up to us.

Danielle later asked how she always seemed to know where we were, as she seemed able to find us at will, no matter the time or place.

"At least she's wearing a coat and scarf," Danielle whispered to me.

A couple were *was* just leaving a bench in the sun and we moved quickly to secure it. Danielle sat so that Natasha would have to sit between us, which she was reluctant to do, but eventually sat.

"I wanted to talk to you about Oleg – Ilya," she said, never one for small talk.

"The funeral was moving," Danielle said.

"Yes, it was beautiful," Natasha agreed. "In spite of everything, he deserved it. He was a good man; he never complained, and he had much to complain about."

"I'm sorry I only met him that once," Danielle said.

There was a pause, and I wanted to get back to the question about the funeral. I knew Natasha was not comfortable with direct questions, so I tried to tease the information out of her.

"I'd never been to an orthodox funeral before," I said. "The cathedral is fascinating, and I wish I knew more of the saints."

Natasha nodded.

"It is beautiful, as is the service. I was pleased that you sat at the back. It meant I could sit with you," she said.

"Do you often attend?" Danielle asked.

"It is too dangerous for me. Those who would harm me are there. I make visits during the day, but to worship, I go to the Greek church in Rue George Bizet."

"Did Ilya – Oleg – have family in Paris?" Danielle asked, bringing Natasha back to the point.

"No. No one. He had to leave them behind. His parents were already dead. Two brothers were killed in the war, and other family was killed during the Revolution."

"He always seemed so cheerful," I said.

"Yes, that was Oleg," Natasha said. "He was glad to be alive, but carried the guilt of the survivor."

That needed no explanation, but while I had always considered Natasha a survivor, I'd never thought about her feelings of guilt.

"That was a pretty elaborate funeral," Danielle continued, on track. "Who arranged it?"

She made no reply for a while.

"You should be more careful about what you want to know," she said at length. "One day you may need to know, but, please do not ask for too much."

She looked at the fallow garden and then around her more generally.

"We are amid places of intrigue and change," she began. "It is fitting. As I told you, there are forces who are trying to rewrite history.

"They are as bad as the Bolsheviks characterise the Imperial family and the aristocrats as villainous parasites who deserved to be exterminated. Just as was done just there," she nodded towards Place de la Concorde.

"Yet, just as then, there were aristocrats who lived up to their moral duties," she continued. "Prince André's father was in charge of vast amounts of land, and André took great interest in them, even when involved in his naval duties. You heard his interest in agriculture yourselves. Anya was the same, and she had even more land. They worked hard to see that there were good managers – but, one cannot be everywhere.

"Poor Oleg was the same. His family did not have as much land, but there must have been a hundred thousand official *desiatinas*. All gone along with beautiful houses in St Petersburg and Moscow."

We waited for Natasha to continue. She was clearly uncomfortable and looking very young and frightened.

"As I told you, there are those who are pretending not to be who they are as well as those who are pretending to be someone they are not. Have you heard of the unknown woman in Germany who they said was Grand Duchess Tatiana?"

We both nodded. The circumstances of the story – a woman fished out of the river confiding in a fellow patient in an asylum – did not engender belief, no matter what the more sensational newspapers alleged.

"She is now supposed to be the Grand Duchess Anastasia," Natasha said. "There are many such people. Some here in Paris. This is what the commission wants to suppress by pretending to be 'authenticating' the various claimants. The irony is, some of those doing the authentication are imposters."

While fond of Natasha, my interest in Russian aristocrats – real or fake – was minimal. Anyone who has ever been in the military has seen enough pretentiousness to last a lifetime, and comes to respect modesty and the ability to do one's job. Danielle had little interest in dubious claims, but did have the interest in people's stories that I did not. It was for these reasons that I liked André and Ilya, not for anything they might have previously been.

"Oleg was real," Natasha continued, "but those who paid for the pomp of his funeral were not. They use such shows of wealth and 'charity' to ingratiate themselves to those who are real, but I am not impressed or deceived.

"I can see through these people, and that is why I am in danger," she said. "And Oleg could see through them, too, and that is why they murdered him."

XXIX
Les Noces III

1925

After that, Danielle was reluctant to press Natasha to attend our wedding and did not mention inviting her again until it was nearly too late.

"I'm sorry, " she said to me. "I regret all that's happened to Natasha, but I won't have murderers that close to my life. My family is here, and we have a business to run. I'm not about to start hiding in doorways and under bridges. Paris is *my home*. Anyway, she will probably show up the way she always does."

I understood Danielle's point of view which is why, after she had declared her intention not to invite Natasha, I never raised the question again. I didn't want murderers in my life again, either.

Natasha, herself, stayed out of our way. I suspect she realised how much she had frightened Danielle. We questioned her about Ilya's death, which I had understood to be an accident while working on the barge, falling, hitting his head and drowning. However, the few news reports, while implying that, were notably short on details.

His death was thought to have occurred at about three in the morning. No one could suggest why he should be up at that time as the barge was due to enter Paris later that morning, and he faced a full day unloading. The examining doctor had also noted that the damage to the skull had been particularly severe, possibly the result of more than one impact. However, in the absence of any other evidence, and a reasonable theory as to why the wound was so deep, the cause of death was recorded as accidental.

That, of course, sufficed for Danielle and me.

We were also otherwise engaged, as it were, and the day was getting closer. Our wedding was a relatively small affair with around forty guests, but I like to think that it was very well done. Danielle and her mother ensured that every detail was correct while her father and I made sure that things happened.

My own parents had embraced Danielle the moment she appeared. I had taken her to Montmirail to meet them and within a few moments, it was clear there would be no problems. They were so eager to see me married that I could have brought home Clytemnestra and they would have welcomed her.

This is not the place for such reminiscences, but we remembered the day fondly and the photographs indicate that people had a good time. Natasha – who encountered us a few days before the event, and was invited by Danielle - avoided all the posed pictures, but a guest took a few less formal ones, and one caught Natasha laughing with Luc and Honorine.

Preparing the new apartment had been time-consuming, and it was a good thing that I had moved in at the beginning of the year as I was able to prevent several major disasters (wrong paint, shelves on the wrong wall among them) before things had got too far along.

We had a short honeymoon (where does one go in February?) in Biarritz before returning to work and the discoveries of never being alone. (My previous taste of this involved several thousand men).

Not surprisingly, we were rather self-absorbed for a while, and it was not until mid-May that we thought about doing more than having the odd meal at the Flamel.

We were also more selective as to which events we went. There were excellent small recitals in various halls and churches, and we visited galleries in the neighbourhood and on the way home rather than go back to the previous ones. We never bought anything, and so would not be missed.

This narrative focuses on Natasha and her circle of artistic, musical and Russian friends and acquaintances, and how we were granted a glimpse into a world that was unknown to us.

Deo gratias, Danielle had a large circle of friends. She had, of course, grown up in Paris and had her web of school friends, many of whom now had husbands. Several of my own school friends now lived in or near Paris, and they, too, were part of what was (for that time and for our economic circumstances) a normal level of social life. I also maintained close acquaintance, if not friendship, with people who had begun as business associates.

There also remained men, like Luc Barnard, whom I had known in the trenches. We tended to encounter each other, rather than seek each other's company, but as the years since the Armistice passed, the need for companions who *knew* grew.

So it was not due to isolation that we went for four months without seeing a single Russian – until Natasha found us in the *Café d'Homme d'Affairs* one Friday evening.

She embraced both of us, something she never did, before sitting down and waving for another glass.

"It's happened," she said, and pulled a copy of that day's *Paris Soir* from her coat.

She folded it open and passed it to us, jabbing an article with her finger.

"See? Just as I told you!"

The article told of the formation of *L'Union de la Noblesse Russe*, and explained how it would list and authenticate claimants. At its head was Prince Vladimir Troubetzkoy.

"He's one of Kirill Vladimirovich's stooges," she said contemptuously.

She had been right about this and Kirill's claim to the throne, and we were curious about how and where she fit into things.

Her wine arrived and she drank half the glass.

"That's not all," she pulled another newspaper from her coat. "This was last week."

Again, she opened and folded the paper to the article she wanted us to see. This was a copy of *Le Figaro*. It was a very short article reporting the death of Francine Gurin, 55, a cook, at a restaurant in the IXth.

"Her name looks French, doesn't it? She was Fryderyka Gurin," Natasha said, pronouncing the name Gureen. "She was a cook at *Kartofel* and a duchess."

"We must have seen her," Danielle said, looked surprised.

"Yes; you did. She cooked that night and helped serve."

"Did you know her well?" Danielle asked.

"In Russia. She knew Orloff, of course. Her father was in the army and would have known André's father," she said. "I also know her well enough to know that she had no heart condition. She was *poisoned* – and *they* did it."

"*Who*?"

"*Охрана!*"

XXX

Охрана

The Okhrana: the word meant nothing to Danielle or me, but we did remember the day several years before when Natasha saw men that had frightened her in a restaurant and made a hasty retreat without explanation. This time, we were not going to let her go before she told us everything.

"It's best you don't know," she said, reaching for her bag.

Danielle had had enough of Natasha's evasions and her sudden appearances that disrupted our lives. Perhaps there was some jealousy at work, too, but she never voiced it.

Gently, but firmly, she put her hand on Natasha's arm and arrested her attempted rise from the chair.

"No!" she said, loudly enough that the couple at the nearest table glanced in our direction.

Natasha returned her bag to the back of the chair and sat down again. She looked shocked and tired. Danielle later told me that she, too, was shocked by the skeletal arm she'd grabbed, but it did not deter her from pressing her advantage.

"Okhrana. What is it? Who are *they*?"

Natasha looked frightened, but resigned, and seeing no escape, nodded to Danielle.

"All right."

Danielle ordered more wine, and Natasha waited until it had come before speaking.

The café was full, and as the evening fell, people moved in from the outside tables. Amid the smoke and the noise, hearing Natasha, who spoke with such a small voice we really had to concentrate. Nevertheless, she got the story out.

The Okhrana was a secret police force for the protection of the tsar and his family. Set up following the attempted assassination of Tsar Alexander II in 1866, it operated across the empire and used what were often described as "unconventional methods" of surveillance, prevention and enforcement. However, even these methods failed to prevent the eventual assassination of Alexander in 1881.

"The Okhrana had branches in several foreign countries," she continued. "Even here in Paris."

"Impossible!" Danielle exclaimed.

"They been here since 1885 to keep an eye on revolutionaries," Natasha said, calmly.

"Do you believe this?" Danielle asked me.

"It's true," Natasha said, simply. "They even worked

with the Sûreté."

"But after the Revolution, with no tsar, it finished?"

Natasha looked at Danielle.

"Oh, no. It remained loyal to the Imperial family. It's still here, and is working for - "

"Kirill," I said.

"Their office was at the Imperial consulate," Natasha said. "97 Rue de Grenelle. They moved, of course, after the Revolution and are in Montmartre. They are now the enforcement arm of those who would control who is who from the old Russia."

"And why is Kirill bad?" Danielle asked.

"After the execution of Tsar Nicholas and his family," here she crossed herself, "his brother became Tsar Mikhail I, but in June 1918, he was murdered by the Bolshevik secret police. Since his body was never found – " here her voice choked and it took a moment for her to recover – "he wasn't declared legally dead until recently. That enabled Kirill to make his move.

"Are you sure you want to know this?" she asked Danielle, again. "What we poor Russians in exile have are three possible tsars, and arguments about it are endless.

"There is Tsar Nicholas II's cousin, Nicholas Nicholaevich; there is Tsar Mikhail's son, George, but he is only fifteen years old and illegitimate; then there is Kirill," she said. "Grand Duke Nicholas was a general and now lives here, just outside Paris. His grandfather was Nicholas I. Nicholas I is Kirill's great, great grandfather."

"That's a very direct line," I said.

"Yes," Natasha agreed. "Nicholas is also much-loved. However, Kirill's grandfather was Alexander III, and his great grandfather was Alexander II, so by primogeniture, he has the rightful claim."

"But, which makes more sense? Two steps to Nicholas I, or four steps to Nicholas I?" I asked.

"Being Russia, there is always another complication," Natasha said. "In 1922, the Zemsky Sobar, the regional parliament of the last outpost of Imperial Russia, declared Nicholas Nicholaevich Tsar of all the Russias. *That* is why the French secret service guards the old Grand Duke, along with some loyal Cossacks," Natasha said, feeling she'd proved her point.

We considered this tangled family squabble.

"Running Okhrana must take a lot of money," I said.

Natasha's laughter rang through the café.

"Do you know who pays for it?" she asked, in a mocking, challenging way. "Russians in the United States. Yes, those people who hated Russia so much that they left decades ago to find a new life in the New World. Ironic, isn't it? They hated Russia, but loved the tsar! Millions of dollars come every year. Okhrana gets the money, and Kirill gets the love."

She told us a few more things including why she thought the Okhrana was behind the deaths of Oleg and the cook/duchess.

I was ready to go home for a cosy supper and sit by the fire, but Danielle suggested we all go to dinner.

"It is not possible," Natasha said. "There isn't time – "

"Of course there is," Danielle said firmly. "You don't have to be at Mme Duflot's until ten. Come!"

Over dinner at a neighbourhood bistro on the way to Mme Duflot's, no more was said of Okhrana, the Imperial Russians, or anything political. Danielle artfully extracted information about Natasha's situation from her.

With the departure of the students from the apartment at the end of term imminent, Natasha would either have to pay more in rent, find new people to share with her for the summer, or move.

"There is no ballet work for a while. One of the productions is a revival, so the costumes are already made," she said.

"What about modelling?" I asked.

"It might come to that," she replied. "The successful artists want young pretty models – which is pointless, because they are unrecognisable in their paintings – and the less successful aren't able to pay much. Though, it's possible to get a place to sleep."

She said all of this without bitterness or regret.

239

"In August, I'll have two weeks with Mademoiselle again. It doesn't pay, but I get room, good food and free lessons for working in the kitchen and doing some cleaning and laundry. It's lovely being there."

We were working our way through a good meal which we were paying inadequate attention to, though amid her narrative, Natasha's enjoyment of it was clear. She commented on it, and Danielle's kindness several times.

&

We still had many questions, and we were both shaken by this theory of Natasha's, mostly because it rang true. That night, in bed, Danielle was genuinely scared. The idea that a murderous foreign agency was at work in Paris with the knowledge and consent of the Sûreté disturbed her sense of order; in a way, she felt betrayed by her own country.

"Do you believe it?" she asked me.

"It seems plausible."

"Oh, don't be so boring! Do you believe her?"

"I don't know," I said. "She appears to know about everything."

She snuggled closer.

"And where do you think she fits? Is she an aristocrat, or just someone who wants to be one?"

That was the question.

"She knows André and Anya; she knows Vladimir

Orloff, whose father was supposed to be the tsar's mother's banker. They all seem to know her – but how could they, if she's lived in Paris since she was six or seven?"

"Perhaps they knew her parents," Danielle suggested.

"And who were they?" I asked.

Danielle shuddered.

"I don't want to know," she said. "I don't want to learn that my country isn't the one I think it is. If that means never seeing Natasha again, well, then, so be it!"

And that's how things were left.

Or so I believed.

The following Friday evening, Natasha was waiting for us outside the office when we came out.

I started to speak, and was worried that Danielle would say something mean to her, but Natasha rushed forward and embraced Danielle, hugging her for nearly a minute.

"Thank you! If I could, I would make you a duchess," she said, then put her finger to her lips, whispered, "Thank you," again, and left us.

"I'm sure there's a story there somewhere," I said.

"Later," said Danielle.

From Natasha's Diary

What is there about this place that makes me want to write? It's almost the only time I do; I think it's because this feels like home, and I feel safe.

Mademoiselle is pleased with my playing. She was happy that I have kept working on the "Toccata" and we are working on some Germaine Tailleferre pieces. I asked Mademoiselle if I could try the Chopin Etude that Anya played before moving to London. She was doubtful, but is letting me try.

I said I feel safe here. I feel safe in my apartment in Paris now, too. I was so frightened after Oleg's death, then Fryderyka's. Oleg used to visit me from the time I was about ten and kept an eye on me. Fryderyka, too, but more distantly. Each year, there are fewer and fewer.

I suppose I have Danielle and Charles, too. It's funny; I had always found her remote. To her, I was Charles's friend; like someone left over from an earlier life. I am sure she was jealous. When she confronted me in the Tuileries and later in the café, I feared I would never see them again. Then, they took me to supper. One day the next week when I went to the apartment when most of the students were out I saw M. Olivier, the landlord. I wanted to *run, but it was too late. I was afraid he was going to ask how I was going to pay for the summer when the students were gone, but he just gave me a receipt that showed my rent paid until the middle of September. I went to my room, stunned with surprise and cried myself to sleep.*

I had been so afraid I'd have to go to the bank again and I am only twenty-two. I do wonder what will become of me. At least Charles and Danielle aren't telling me to get married. They look very happy and comfortable with each other.

One day last week, an American was here and Mademoiselle spent the whole day with him. People were standing in the courtyard by the open window listening to them playing to each other. Such sounds they were making! Eventually, Mademoiselle stuck her head out and told us to get back to work, but promised that they would play for us in the evening.

After supper, we crowded into the room with the two pianos and they played a piece he called Rhapsodie en Bleu. *I'm not sure it's serious music, but a welcome change from Stravinsky.*

Mme Mercier is only able to come downstairs for a short period each day, so Sandra is much happier now, even though she has to do more work, taking meals up to her mother and looking after her. I can't believe how much Sandra's cooking has improved. Probably because her mother isn't there to inhibit her.

There's usually some time to walk in the countryside. It's one of the few memories I have of Russia, but whether it was outside Moscow or St Petersburg, I don't know. I do remember the trains between them; sleeping in wooden compartments with velvet curtains. Blossom in the spring, and a "flowery boulevard"; where was that, I wonder.

Sandra and I gathered elderberries, blackberries and raspberries. She also picked some sloes, talking all the while about other fruit that was nearly ready. We had apples and grapes at most meals and she could make pastry faster than anyone I knew. I did teach her an old Russian trick: put vodka in your pastry; it makes it smoother to work with, gives a better texture, and doesn't affect the taste. She will make a good man a wonderful wife.

XXXI
A Lesson in Russian History

1925

Somehow, Danielle made the transition to married life much more easily than I did. She was instantly open, sharing her thoughts and feelings. Although there was nothing I wanted to hide from her, I found sharing difficult. Danielle told me about paying Natasha's rent as though it were the most natural thing to do.

"She has no family; no one to look after her," Danielle said. "She wouldn't have taken the money had I offered it to her, so just paying the rent was the easiest thing."

"I wasn't even sure you *liked* her," I said. "I thought you only tolerated her because of the way we met."

"Oh, Charles. Is that really what you think?" she asked in near despair at my ability to understand what was to her obvious. "I'm lucky she says anything to me."

"Why's that?"

She stared at me in frustrated disbelief.

"Do you not think she wanted you for herself?"

It was my turn to gape at her.

"Natasha made it clear to me from the start that that wasn't a possibility," I said.

"All girls say that," she retorted.

"Well, I know I don't understand women, but the only slightly romantic things she's *ever* said to me were about you, and how I shouldn't let you get away!"

Danielle looked dumbstruck.

"She said that?" she asked eventually, her voice just above a whisper.

"More than once," I said. "We weren't alone that much; you were usually with me."

Danielle's eyes were actually filled with tears. I'd never seen that before. I put my arms around her and held her close.

"If I'd known that, I would have done more for her," she said. "We must continue to help her."

"Let's be sensible," I said. "We've known her for four years and know nothing about her. I don't think she's a confidence trickster, but I don't think she's normal."

"*You* lose your parents, your friends and your country and see how normal *you'd* be!" Danielle exclaimed. "Yes, she can be exasperating, but the least we can do is see that she has a safe place to live. Do you want her sleeping with people just to have a place to stay?"

I was greatly surprised by the vehemence of Danielle's words; at the same time, I never loved her more. Her principled courage – especially to someone she had considered a possible rival – was admirable.

"I know we have no way of getting in touch with her,

but when she turns up, we must make sure she's fed. Maybe one day we can visit one of the stores," she said. "We're not princes or duchesses, but we have enough to be comfortable and can afford to do a few things."

Danielle always knew I'd wanted to help Natasha, but she'd never understood that I didn't want anything from her, though I think, after a short time, Natasha had come to realise that.

We discussed helping her find a job, but apart from sewing and playing the piano, we had no real idea what Natasha could do.

"I can't see her working in a shop," Danielle said. "Not unless she had a whole new wardrobe and hair style. And I don't know if she has any commercial sense."

I only worried for a moment that Natasha would become a project or an obsession with Danielle. However, her common sense prevailed and, while she continued to assist her, it was done with care and imagination, so she was unable to refuse.

We had expected to see Natasha in the weeks before Christmas. We hadn't done much apart from work, and Danielle was eager to cook Christmas dinner for her parents in our flat. She wasn't a bad cook but cooking hadn't been a priority or an interest. She was a businesswoman, after all.

The day was a success. M. Doré who would have been

happy with a *croque monsieur* pronounced himself more than satisfied with the goose, four vegetables, cake, tartes and a cream compote of some sort. Three bottles of wine helped, too. Mme Doré, once ushered out of the kitchen, was pleasantly surprised with her daughter's achievement.

We had agreed to invite Natasha, but she was nowhere to be found. Danielle and I had called at her apartment and left a note, it wasn't until late January 1926 that she revealed herself.

She looked well and we soon found out why.

"I've been in England," she said. "Uncle André and Anya invited me. I travelled with one of his company directors who was returning to London. I went on the night ferry where they put the whole train on the ferry. It was very exciting."

She told us about being taken to concerts, visiting the National Gallery and seeing the sights.

"While it was wonderful to see André and Anya, I wanted to see a lady called Larissa Tudor who lives deep in Kent with her husband," she said, her voice growing serious.

"I wanted to warn her about the Okhrana and Kirill's usurpation of power."

We must have looked confused, and Natasha stopped and explained.

"You said you'd heard of Anna Tchaikovsky who is claiming to be one of the Grand Duchesses. I said there were others. Larissa Feodorovna – or rather her husband – believes she is the Grand Duchess Tatiana. Indeed, she is very beautiful and her colouring is the same, but I wouldn't know how true the belief is. It is amusing to think that a Romanoff is a Tudor."

She paused, seemingly to think about the lady.

"And she needs to be warned?"

"Yes, she is in danger; ironically, because she is not making any claims loudly. It's a quiet belief – a special knowledge – that she and her husband seem to have. That is more suspicious than Anna 'Anastasia' Tchaikovsky who refuses to speak Russian and whose French isn't good. Larissa's Russian is beautiful, and that puts her in danger."

"But how would – "

"No. No more; it could put us all in danger," she said. "Tell me about your first Christmas together . . . ."

୨୦

Danielle was able to get a little more information by asking about London and the night train. Such things were beyond our experience.

In telling us about the journey, she revealed that she had been smuggled onto the train as she had no passport, and feared being seen. In the bustle of boarding, she moved from the carriage where servants travelled, to the director's private compartment where she spent the night folded into the upper berth where she remained until they reached the outskirts of London whereupon she'd re-joined the servants in third class.

She panicked slightly after telling us, and made excuses about how poor Russians have doubtful papers but that she needed to warn Larissa urgently.

Danielle and I discussed this at some length over the coming weeks.

"Why should Natasha feel that *she* should be the one to warn Larissa?" I wondered.

We'd speculated on theories many times before, but Danielle felt we had more to go on.

"Why is this so important to her?"

Danielle's best theory was that she had had some proximity to a part of the Imperial family, most likely as a maid or some servant.

"Someone close enough to pick up their education and manners," she said. "There were lots of cousins, she could have been in their households. That would explain her good French, knowledge of the family, and manners."

"But not her piano playing."

XXXII

Manifestations

1926

It was hard to believe the increase of business experienced by Moreau, Doré et Cie. In March, the partners had a discussion with Danielle and me about expanding the numbers and fulfilling the promotions that had been deferred at our request.

Curiously, I was the cautious one who didn't want the company to over-reach itself and suggested that the expansion be phased in, with Danielle – who had several years more experience than I – stepping up her position.

This was agreed, and as part of a celebration, we went to a Koussevitzky concert at the end of May. We did not see Natasha, or anyone we knew there, though Danielle's parents and the Moreaus knew a number of the members of the audience. There was, I thought, a rather non-descript piano concerto by a Pole named Tansman, who also played it. The memorable piece was the Brahms fourth symphony, which I had heard once before during the war. The power and emotion of the piece was nearly overwhelming and the impression it created remained with us for many days.

Several days after that, Natasha found us and told us

that we should see the controversial new Ballet Russes production of *Romeo et Juliette*. She had worked on the costumes with a Spanish artist called Nero, which sounded slightly sinister.

Natasha looked well; the ballet had been busy, so she was working steadily and Mme Duflot's remained popular. She had even tried doing some sketches and watercolours herself.

"Since seeing *Les Biches* two years ago, I've loved Marie Laurencin's ethereal paintings," she said. "The first hundred I did were terrible, but they're good now."

I had learned that Natasha's directness was a symptom of her process of simultaneous translation, not vanity. She had never indicated that she considered herself better than anyone else.

When we met her at the Théâtre Sarah Bernhardt, she was excited about the evening.

"It will be another like *Les Noces*," she exclaimed happily.

"I hope not," I whispered to Danielle.

In many ways, it was worse.

There had been much controversy about the production and there were crowds in Place du Châtelet to see – or participate – in any *manifestation*. We nearly had to push our way to the entrance. The mood of the crowd was mostly jovial, but we knew this could change quickly.

Danielle clutched her handbag firmly and I kept close track of my watch and wallet.

On entering, we saw no one we knew but recognised faces from previous concerts and performances. We had managed to get good seats slightly to the right in the first balcony and had an excellent view of the stage and much of the house. A bright, odd curtain hung which our programme showed was by a German "surrealist" named Max Ernst, while the set and costumes were done by a Spanish surrealist called Miro, my previous understanding having been erroneous. Having seen the curtain, I suspected the sets and costumes would also be unconventional.

Constant Lambert was a very young Englishman whom Diaghilev had commissioned to write the piece. I thought the music, though pleasant, rather dull. In fact, the whole ballet was about as dull as it could have been.

The real entertainment was in the house where, as soon as the curtain went up, people in the top balcony dumped leaflets on the audience below, and shouts and calls began. Someone was blowing a whistle, and through out the ballet, there were similar disruptions and several scuffles.

We felt safe where we were, two rows back and so not in danger of being pushed over the edge, though when people near us began shouting, we did feel uncomfortable.

255

"Art is not for capitalists!" was one of the chants, though what this political protest had to do with Romeo or Juliette, we had no idea. It was later explained to us that a group of surrealists – and we had little idea who or what *they* were – felt that Ernst and Miro had caved in to capitalism by being associated with the filthy commercialism of Diaghilev and the Ballet Russes.

When we left the theatre, it seemed that there were almost as many police as protesters, and we all milled together as we spilled onto the street.

Natasha came up to us, glowing with excitement.

"Wasn't it wonderful!" she exclaimed. "Diaghilev arranged for the police himself. It will be wonderful publicity and ensure full houses for the run."

As a piece of theatre, it was an interesting evening, but artistically – well, I had been spoiled by *Les Mariés de la Tour Eiffel*, *Within the Quota* and *Le Train Bleu*. The irony was, none of them was Russian.

⁂

Business was cruising at a comfortable pace and people were beginning to discuss their holidays. The previous summer, Danielle and I had what we called Part II of our honeymoon and had gone to a hotel near the beach at Arcachon.

This year, we'd be going with Danielle's parents to the guest house in Deauville that I had been to two summers earlier. Her parents had been discussing where to go when I mentioned the place in Deauville. Danielle giggled when her parents suggested we join them, and this suddenly didn't seem like a holiday. However, it was clear that Danielle liked the idea, and she placated me by saying we could escape for meals on our own, go for long walks, or simply pretend to be out.

It was a week after the *Romeo et Juliette* fiasco that Natasha met us outside the office in tears. How long she'd been waiting in the street was hard to tell, but her tears were fresh. It was nearly seven when we emerged from the office, anticipating a quiet evening with a piece of fish and a bottle of wine.

Danielle embraced her and began leading her down the street. She sensed that we were headed to *Café L'Homme d'Affaires*, and asked if we could go to the *Jardin du Palais Royale*.

She clung to Danielle, but stopped crying.

We found seats and Danielle soaked a handkerchief in the fountain and set to work on Natasha's face. She offered no resistance. She had been hyperventilating but her breathing was now slowing down and she was soon able to talk.

"There was a woman called Michelle Anches," she began. "She was one of the claimants who opposed Kirill. She had moved around Siberia before coming to Paris last year."

As she told the story, she seemed to become calmer, so we encouraged her to continue.

"Michelle claimed to be Grand Duchess Tatiana. She was the same age, and several of the Imperial cousins believed her claim," she continued. "For years she tried to meet the Dowager Duchess, Maria Feodorovna, and a meeting was finally arranged in Denmark.

"On Wednesday, she was due to leave Paris and travel to see the duchess, but she was murdered in her home Tuesday night."

She finished this sensational narrative in seeming calm, but as she looked to us for our reaction, she burst into tears again.

"Do you think *that's* a coincidence? They are closing in: the Okhrana."

XXXIII

Angels at the Portal of Judgement

1926

For a moment, I thought there were going to be two women in tears. Danielle looked as terrified as Natasha as she tried to take in the implications of what she had heard.

To my relief, but not to my surprise, Danielle recovered quickly and returned to the task of calming down Natasha. This was not easy, because as Natasha herself had noted, Michelle Anches's death did not look like a coincidence.

Danielle stood and we walked down the Rue de Rivoli with Natasha. We'd stop to look in windows and chat briefly before moving on. I was reminded of my first walk with Natasha and mentioned it to her.

She smiled.

"I had no idea that I'd still know you years later," she said. "My acquaintances tend to be brief."

"I remember looking in the window of an antique shop with you," I began.

Danielle was listening closely as I had not told her much about that evening; I sometimes wondered what she may have speculated.

"You asked me what the most interesting thing I could see was," Natasha said.

"You remember," I said with a laugh.

"What did you say?" Danielle asked her.

Natasha looked at me.

"Do *you* remember?" she asked.

"Of course. You said, 'Our reflections.'"

Danielle stared at her.

"No wonder he wanted to keep in touch with you," she said in amazement. "I said a desk."

Natasha laughed and put her arm through Danielle's.

"I wish I could be as practical as you," she said, affectionately.

We continued to walk. I guessed it was Danielle's intention to walk Natasha back to her apartment. We had passed the Tour Saint Jacques and were crossing *Pont Notre Dame*. We paused to watch a barge stacked with barrels pass beneath the bridge, and we were all reminded of Ilya. Natasha's mood dropped again, but Danielle surprised both of us.

As we came into the square before Notre Dame, Danielle moved toward the cathedral and stopped about a hundred feet from the doors.

"The central doorway is the Portal of the Last Judgement," she explained. "The ranks of figures decorating the archivolts are angels, saints, prophets and Biblical figures."

I was wondering where this impromptu tour was leading us, but Natasha seemed interested.

"Look at the doors themselves but be aware of the angels," she instructed. "Don't stare at anything in particular and be patient."

I only half complied, but Natasha did as she was told as Danielle waited.

Presently, Natasha squealed and turned to Danielle with a big smile.

"It's wonderful!" she laughed. "How does it work?"

Danielle returned the smile.

"I have no idea," she said. "My father showed me when I was about eight. It always works. I wonder who first discovered it, and when."

"It's wrong to under-estimate people in history," Natasha said. "Wait. I'm going to do it again."

This time I joined in, albeit sceptically. Yet, to my amazement, an angel seemed to jump up the archivolt. I continued to watch until two more had mischievously swapped positions.

"I am sorry I ever doubted you," I said, turning to Danielle, bowing and kissing her hand.

Natasha laughed, and we continued across *Pont de Coeurs* and turned on to Quai de Montebello before moving away from the river.

As we were crossing Boulevard Saint Germain, Danielle suggested we find somewhere to eat.

"It is not necessary for you to walk me all the way home," Natasha said. "I know I've behaved like a child, but I am not one."

"You were frightened," Danielle said. "And, when we are frightened, we behave like children, no matter how old we are."

"You are both very patient with me," she said.

Natasha was happier and less nervous after her meal and several glasses of wine, and we walked her to the Rue du Cardinal Lemoine.

"We'll wait across the street for five minutes, so if anything is amiss, scream," I said.

Danielle struck my arm.

"Don't encourage her," she said.

We waited and there was no scream, just a wave from an upper hallway window.

◌

A late influx of business combined with preparations to decamp to Deauville for three weeks filled our time. We substituted walks in one of the parks or along the river for visits to galleries and the theatre.

Paris was very warm and uncomfortable and we were looking forward to sea air. Danielle was particularly eager to get away. She had taken on her new responsibilities in the office with efficiency and total competence. By now, no one in Paris was remarking at women performing jobs that had previously been done by men. With few men, there was no choice, and the country was not suffering from the change.

We were due to take the train to Deauville on Saturday, August 7, and had been working long days to wrap things up. The office couldn't be closed completely, and a skeleton staff would meet urgent requirements (for a supplemental charge) and deal with any problems with shipping and deliveries. Those people would then go on holiday when we returned.

On the Wednesday before our departure, Danielle and I had a feeling of *déja vu* when we left the building and found Natasha in a distressed state.

After holding her for a few moments, we automatically walked to the Jardin du Palais Royale and sat by the fountain.

Once seated and her face wiped, she continued shaking for another few minutes before Danielle could get any sense out of her. She looked exhausted and probably hadn't eaten for a while. In the heat and light of summer, Natasha looked very pale and thin.

"We cannot help you unless you tell us something," Danielle said, gently.

Natasha wiped her eyes again and took a few breaths

then reached into her handbag and pulled out a piece of paper, folded and crumpled.

She unfolded it and passed it to me.

The writing was beautiful copperplate, evenly written on both sides in rich black ink. The paper was a good quality ivory stock. I focused on the signature.

"It's from André," I said to Danielle. "But, it's in Russian. What does it say, Natasha?"

"Larissa is dead," she said, gathering her wits. "I warned her. Poor Frederick will be devastated. He loved her so much, and she was so beautiful."

"Larissa, the claimant?" I asked, and Natasha nodded.

"I *warned* her," she repeated.

She took the letter and read it.

"*My dearest Natasha, it is my unhappy duty to tell you that Larissa Feodorovna Tudor died on July 18. The cause of her death was given as pulmonary tuberculosis,*" she managed to read. "The rest of the letter is about his work, his hopes for my happiness and concerns for my safety."

Her tears were finished, and she just sat, as if in a daze.

Danielle stood and walked to the edge of the fountain. I followed.

"We should take her home," she whispered.

"Like last time?"

"No. To our apartment. She can sleep on the sofa; the other room is full of our trunks and clothes," she said.

"She can have supper with us."

Natasha was not suspicious of where we were going until we failed to cross the river. Danielle explained the plan, which she resisted, nearly violently.

"Would you stop us from offering this kindness?" she asked. "You'll be fed; you can sleep and you'll be safe."

She was again about to protest, but seeing the resolve on both our faces, conceded.

I had no doubt she knew exactly where we lived, after all, she had found me at the Flamel. Actually bringing her into our home was another matter, but Danielle had no doubts.

We had a simple meal during which Natasha was virtually silent. Danielle and I spoke about work and plans for the weekend. After supper, we sat in easy company, finishing the wine and enjoying a coffee. Natasha, of course, had tea and Danielle gave her jam without being reminded.

We could see that Natasha was fading and retired early.

When we said goodnight, she simply replied, "Thank you."

When we rose in the morning, she was gone.

ഔ

"I feel very sorry for her, but I don't want any more of this Russian novel playing out in my life," Danielle said, wearily. "Let's just get through today and tomorrow and forget everything."

I echoed her sentiments and we said no more about Natasha. At least she had not mentioned the Okhrana which would have upset Danielle far more than she had been.

We saw no more of Natasha that week, and on a bright Saturday morning, loaded our luggage into a taxi and went to Gare Saint-Lazare where we met Danielle's parents. The number of cases and trunks was daunting, but there were two baggage cars on the train and plenty of taxis when we arrived at Deauville.

To my relief, the hotel was much as it was when I had been there before, and it suited the Dorés very well. Danielle delivered on her promise of escaping on our own, and our time there passed both pleasantly and quickly.

Natasha's Diary

August 1926

It took me several days to feel safe here at Mademoiselle's. My apartment is empty for the summer, André and Anya are gone, and Charles and Danielle are away. I miss them so much. I don't see them often, and I am always a burden to them, but without their kindness I don't know what I would have done, and I feel that because I know them, I am safer.

I am sad because this has been a very good year with my good fortune of Danielle's generosity, some good work with the ballet, and, of course, the steady demands of Mme Duflot's clientele. Against this, are the continuing deaths and the strengthening of Kirill's grip even on my exile.

One of my happier predictions is coming true: Sandra is engaged and will be married shortly after Christmas. I have met him, he works on a farm between here and Brueil-en-Vexin, a few miles away. He seems nice and they are very happy; I'm happy for them, even though she slips out during the evening and I have to do more work. As if to compensate, Sandra has made strawberry jam and given me a jar for my tea.

My piano playing is just as Mademoiselle describes:

technically sound, but musically unsteady. She knows there is something wrong with me but does not pry, and I do not wish to burden her, too.

We've been working on Mozart; Mademoiselle thinks it will help my discipline, but she's also given me a piece to work on by one of her American composer friends, a short "blues" piece with the unhelpful marking "freely poetic." Don't today's composers know how they want a piece to sound?

I am trying to decide whether to tell my story to Charles and Danielle. Of all the people I know, they deserve to know it; also, they would be the ones least in danger from knowing. I would have to trust them more than I've ever trusted anyone. In Paris, only Aunt Olga knew for sure, and she's dead. Charles and Danielle would think I am mad like the Tchaikovsky woman, but perhaps they will see how it makes sense of everything else.

When I arrived, both Sandra and her mother said I needed fattening up; it's the first thing I've ever heard them agree on.

XXXIV
Winter Dreams

1926

One of the things Danielle and I discussed sitting by the sea and enjoying the evening light was how Natasha had caused our lives to revolve around Russians. We decided to make more of an effort to see more French artists, musicians and films. We knew we'd enjoyed Poulenc, Milhaud and their friends, but though stunning, we wanted a change from Koussevitzky, Stravinsky and Prokofiev. Studying the season's concert programme, we saw that was going to be even more difficult with Rachmaninoff and Glazunov in Paris, at least intermittently.

Instead of the typically gradual resumption of business after the holidays, we were exceptionally busy from the time we returned until nearly mid-October. Crop failures in one country and surpluses in another were part of the normal rhythm of our work, but disruptions in transport had compounded shortages that could have normally been accommodated. There was no particular reason for this, it was the simple concurrence of isolated events that resulted in a succession of new logistical arrangements having to be made.

We were glad not to have the added distraction of

further Russian assassinations and *coups d'etat*, though in May, the head of the Ukranian government in exile had been murdered on the pavement of Rue Racine, near Boulevard Saint Michel. Reports were that it was a simple murder, and the absence of Natasha suggesting it was an Okhrana killing gave us the assurance that the death was as described in the press.

Still, we missed Natasha and hoped she was all right.

"Why don't we try visiting her?" Danielle suggested on Friday. "We could call at her apartment on the way to a café in the area. Maybe go for a walk in the Luxembourg Gardens."

I wanted to know she was well but was reluctant to present myself at her apartment. Who knew what went on in student apartments these days?

Danielle eventually persuaded me and around noon time Saturday, we climbed to the top of the Rue du Cardinal Lemoine building and knocked on her door. It was opened by a well-presented young man who was friendly, if wary.

Danielle explained who we were and he agreed to fetch Natasha. He didn't invite us in, but put the chain on the door while we waited.

When she saw who it was, she removed the chain and embraced Danielle with big smiles. She was wearing one of her old-fashioned dresses and was only slightly less pale than the last time we'd seen her.

"We thought we'd see if you'd like to join us for lunch," Danielle said, after Natasha had greeted me.

"Do you know *Le Cercle*? On the corner of Saint-Michel and Rue Gay Laussac, just opposite the gardens," she said. "I'll be there in a quarter of an hour. I've been painting and need to clean up."

We found the café easily and took places with a view of the gardens. Natasha arrived, still looking happy, and hugging us. She sat and lit a cigarette.

"You are still painting?" I asked.

"Yes – but actually, I mis-spoke earlier; I wasn't painting, I was being painted."

"Did we interrupt?" Danielle asked. "You should have said – "

"It's all right," Natasha replied waving her hand. "Thomas, who answered the door, is a medical student, but he also wants to do medical illustrations. He's very good; I model for anatomy drawing practice."

"That's fine until he wants to paint dissections," I managed to say before Danielle hit my arm lightly with the back of her hand.

Natasha, who had seen this many times, laughed.

"Today he was drawing my skull," she said. "He's trying to look beneath the skin, flesh and muscle to draw the skull. He can get the basic shapes by looking, but the rest

271

is done by touch."

"How was Gargenville?" Danielle asked before Natasha's lack of discretion manifested itself too graphically.

She told us of her weeks in the country and the various characters that had come to play and compose. She chatted about walks, practising the piano, and Sandra's fiancé.

"You are looking happy," I said. "A bit pale, but happier than we've seen you for a while."

I think she blushed. She finished her cigarette and took a drink. Danielle and I waited for her to say something.

She stubbed out the cigarette.

"One doesn't like to tempt fate," she said.

We continued to wait; Danielle's judgement on such things was near-perfect.

"There is work with the ballet," Natasha began. "Mme Duflot's continues to be popular, and I have been doing a lot of painting. There's a little man by the Quai Voltaire who hangs a few of my watercolours. Thomas says there's a stall near Austerlitz that has a lot of modern pictures and I might do better there."

Danielle turned to me and winked at the mention of Thomas, making no effort to conceal the gesture from Natasha.

We waited again for her to continue. She fiddled with

her wine glass, took out another cigarette and went through a series of poses while lighting it. When she'd done all that and exhaled, the waiter appeared to take our food order.

Danielle gave ours quickly and Natasha pretended to change her mind and look at the menu again, but the no-nonsense waiter solved her indecision by saying, "I think madam would like the fish."

We laughed, as seeing Natasha *not* in charge of things was very rare.

It looked like we were going to play the waiting game again, but Danielle spoke.

"Enough, Natasha. It's time to talk."

The look she gave us was possibly the most endearing expression we'd ever seen from her. She smiled, looked meek and girlish and twisted her fingers.

"He's very nice," she said, finally.

"*Nice*?! Is that all you can say?" Danielle demanded.

Natasha laughed, now used to her bluffs.

"He's very patient," she said, laughing. "He has to be to cope with me."

We waited for her to continue, but Danielle had to prompt her.

"Tell us, Natasha. From the beginning."

She put out the half-smoked cigarette.

"He is one of the students in the apartment this term,"

she began. "He's a second year medical student. He was in the apartment when I returned from Gargenville."

"He's quite good looking," Danielle said, hoping to shake loose some more information.

"He's from near Lyons, and I think he's very clever," she said. "Since we were together on our own, we cooked for each other and went out for drinks and the odd meal.

"One day, I found the sitting room covered in anatomical sketches and text books. He's done hundreds of drawings," she said. "He didn't want to talk about them, but I told him I'd been a model and showed him some of my watercolours. He pretended he liked them, and told me about the stall near Austerlitz."

This was the most I'd ever heard her say, yet, she gave very little away.

Danielle reached over to her and took her hand.

"Alas," she said to me. "No ring yet."

"It will be Christmas soon," I said.

Natasha laughed, but was clearly embarrassed.

"We are *friends*," she said. "We are getting to be better friends, but we cannot be more than that unless I tell him about myself. I am not prepared to risk that just now."

It looked as though her pseudo-imperial disposition was going to stand in the way of happiness once again. Then, her face lit up as she saw the food arrive, and *that* stood in the way of Danielle and me learning any more.

XXXV

L'après-midi au cinéma

1926

Our expectations remained unfulfilled as Natasha refused to share more information. Danielle shifted her attention from trying to find out more about Thomas to trying to understand what Natasha was so reluctant to tell him.

"Anyone who is close to an exile, refugee, *émigré*, or whatever you want to call yourself is going to have an unconventional story," Danielle said. "Real friends are more interested in what you are and what you will become than in what you were or what you might have done."

"That is why you are so dear to me," Natasha said. "You never pry, but only care about my well-being and happiness."

Danielle was, curiously, not moved by this sentimentality.

"If you want someone to care for you – I mean *really* care for you – you must be honest with them," she said. "If, having heard your story, they can't love you, then they are not for you."

Natasha was surprised by this confrontation and retreated into her more usual reserved self.

"It is not that I can't see the wisdom of what you say, but suppose telling that story puts them and me in danger? What would you do then?" she asked.

The question was punctuated by a sudden clap of thunder and an instant downpour that sent the crowds scuttling for shelter. We were well-under the awning and unless the wind picked up, we were dry, but those farther down on the pavement rushed inside carrying what they could.

"Love is about giving someone else the power to possibly hurt you," Danielle said. "It's always a risk, but the bigger the risk, the bigger the reward."

"Or danger," Natasha said, looking straight into Danielle's eyes.

"But you have to weigh the life you could lead against the one you're leading," Danielle persisted. "Sometimes, it's a way out of a corner."

Natasha nodded.

"What do you want to do since it's raining," I asked when we had finished our meals.

Danielle and I were drinking coffee while Natasha had her black tea with jam.

"There's a cinema near here," she said. "They may have something starting soon."

When the rain slowed to a heavy drizzle for a few minutes, we made our move, following Natasha to the

Cinema du Panthéon. A film based on the Zola novel, *Nana*, would be starting in about fifteen minutes, so we went in. I had read the novel during the war, but had only a vague recollection. It was, however, as I remembered, a tale about a girl from the Paris slums who wants to escape her life and has an affair with an important government official in the hopes of rising to his status, but, of course, the reverse happens.

Given our conversation with Natasha, I wondered if this would be the afternoon escape she wished.

Coming out into the light after a film is always disorientating as one re-enters the real world. I was still adjusting while Natasha was enthusiastically chattering on about it, saying it had reminded her of Russian literature. She kept up her monologue all the way back to her apartment where we left her.

~

Danielle was quiet as we returned home after leaving Natasha. I didn't know if she was thinking about the film, or Natasha, or if I had said or done something wrong. Whatever the cause, I knew she would speak when she was ready.

Later when she was cooking dinner, I poured her a glass of wine. She came from the kitchen and sat at our small dining table.

"What could she tell someone that would put them in

danger?" she asked. "We've always known she has secrets, but I'd always thought they were ones she was keeping for other people."

"I thought that after she'd invited us to meet André and Anya that she might open up more," I said. "The deaths of Ilya and the cook, and then the two pretenders have really shaken her."

"Yet, she remains in Paris."

"Practically in hiding," I added.

We wondered whether Thomas would bring her out of herself more. She clearly felt affection for him, and it was the first indication we'd had that she cared for anyone.

Danielle was looking unhappy.

"You can't make people be happy," I said, knowing that saying the wrong thing was very easy. "She may feel that the best part of her life was in Russia. It may have been."

Danielle looked at me, and her pain was evident.

"That is the most depressing thing I've heard," she whispered.

"If she doesn't want to be saved, you won't be able to do it."

୧

It took a few days for the gloom to lift from Danielle. Work helped, as did a meal out on Friday night, but when the weather was miserable on Saturday, I proposed another trip to the cinema.

I was surprised how readily Danielle acceded to the suggestion, and we made our way to Boulevard Poissonnière to the Cine-Max Linder to see *Le Diable au Corps*. I had read that book during the war, too, but disappointingly there was no connection between the film and the book.

I thought the cinema with its two balconies more remarkable than the film. However, Danielle enjoyed it, and was more cheerful when we emerged into daylight. The weather had improved somewhat, but it was still overcast and very cold. We walked around the corner to *Chartier* for a late lunch.

We were able to be seated immediately, but it was still very busy with Christmas shoppers and people like us who were looking for something to do in the depressing weather.

Danielle talked about the film, the actors, and then brought the conversation around to what I suspected had been on her mind for some time.

"Do you mind being ordinary?"

I could guess where this came from, but understanding why women asked this sort of question was something I never grasped. A man, unless he is unusually ambitious, treats life as a series of duties, adventures, rewards, trials, and other successes or impediments but generally considers himself to be what he is. There are dreams and stratagems, but by and large, we are content, otherwise we would not be doing what we're doing where we're doing it.

Not counting being in the army, of course. Then, one was simply glad to be breathing in the morning. Also, in our own heads, we are never ordinary, and believe that in the world there are people who like us and those who do not.

Men also have an impish nature that leads them to say things they shouldn't regardless of the consequences. (See above: those who like us, and those who do not.)

I pretended to consider the question for half a second before replying.

"Do you think *I* am ordinary?"

Had our meals been delivered, I am sure a plate would have been speeding towards my head, given Danielle's expression.

"Charles, I'm being serious," she said, almost pleading. "We get up, we go to work; we go out to eat; we go to a concert, a gallery, a film; we see our friends; but are we just watching? Should we be *doing* more?"

There's nothing like sitting in the dark for two hours watching people do things while you're not to foster doubt and discontentment. I had thought Danielle was above such self-doubt. Now that we were married, I had hoped she'd overcome her insecure fears of lifetime spinsterhood.

"Are you feeling trapped?" I asked, hoping she'd find some empathy in my tone.

She shrugged.

"Do you need me to tell you here how much I've grown to love you? How I admire you at work? How others view your abilities?" I asked.

This at least provoked a blush, which was as exceptional an occurrence for her as it was for Natasha.

Our meals arrived while she was considering how to react.

"Let me put it this way, who do you know – friend, acquaintance, someone famous – that you would really like to trade places with?"

I refilled her wine glass. She started to speak, but her instinctive thoughtfulness asserted itself, as did the aroma of the *pavé* that had just been placed before her.

"*Bon appétit*," she said.

XXXVI
Celebrations

1926-1927

We had enjoyed the time around Christmas and New Year's and had shared many meals with friends and Danielle's parents and mine. People kept appearing at our apartment or telephoning us to arrange to visit. While there were no big parties, there was a succession of gatherings, planned and unplanned, that kept us busy, even on days of normal work.

Natasha had not appeared, although we had invited her to share Christmas day with us, even to attend midnight Mass at Notre Dame des Blanc-Mantaux. Saint Nicholas-des-Champs was equidistant from the apartment, but Danielle liked the brightness of Notre Dame, so we went there, even though it was midnight. The music was glorious, and the priest stuck to the Biblical texts and didn't warn of the evils of gluttony and drunkenness.

The streets were busy almost all the way home, and though freezing cold, the city lights and the good-humoured pedestrians – whether returning from churches, restaurants or private parties – made the night feel special.

I unlocked the door, turned on the lights and opened

the vent to the stove to warm up the room.

"Would you like a glass of something?" I asked Danielle.

"A brandy to warm up would be lovely," she said.

I was happy to see her looking healthy and content. Her cheeks were red from the cold, and she sat on the sofa near the fire with her overcoat on.

"I half expected to see Natasha when we came out of church," she said. "It's a pity she wouldn't come for lunch."

"I have given up trying to understand her. Anyway, she won't be celebrating Christmas until the seventh."

Danielle sat back and opened her coat and drank some brandy.

"She'll be celebrating with the Greeks," she said. "She is so afraid of going to the Russian cathedral. Even if people were looking for her – which I doubt – how would they recognise her? I think she has a vivid imagination, and daydreams that are in danger of running – and ruining – her life."

I sat next to her and we touched glasses.

"*Joyeux Noël*, darling."

"*Joyeux Noël*."

࿗

Danielle's parents came for lunch with a neighbour of theirs whom they had known for decades. Mme Arnaud was a widow and like an aunt to Danielle. A dignified woman with a good sense of style, Mme Arnaud said remarkably little, but would come out with unexpected and pithy comments that amused everyone.

We ate and drank for a good part of the afternoon and in the following satisfied stupor, sat by the fire and exchanged a few small presents. Danielle gave me the latest volume of Proust, and I gave her a long, brightly coloured silk scarf with a modernist design.

When they left, we followed them down to the street. They would find a taxi in Rue du Temple. When we returned to our apartment, we found a rectangular parcel wrapped in brown paper and tied with string next to the door.

Danielle picked it up and took it inside and set about untying the knots. When she unwrapped it, we found two small framed watercolours.

"There's a note," I said, pointing to the floor by Danielle's feet where it had fallen.

"*With thanks from the heart for your many kindnesses, Love, Natasha,*" she read.

We looked at them and recognised influences of different painters we had seen in the past few years, but they were most like Marie Laurencin.

"Do you know what Natasha says about Marie Laurencin?" I asked.

Danielle shook her head.

"She says that you can tell who she's sleeping with by the style of painting she's doing," I said.

Though not prudish, Danielle had little time for the prurient, but laughed quite freely.

"I'm not going to analyse the styles of these too closely," she said. "I think they are lovely and you can hang them tomorrow."

We knew that Natasha would have left them at the door while we were eating and were disappointed that she did not make her presence known.

"It means I'll have to carry her present with me all the time," Danielle said. "Since she never lets us know her intentions, I can't plan."

"It's a good thing it's a small parcel," I said.

We hadn't given Natasha presents before we were married; I reckoned she had enough in the way of meals and drinks, but last year, Danielle wanted to give her something.

We'd had a long discussion about what she would not feel uncomfortable receiving, and one evening after stopping for a coffee at *Le Boeuf sur la Toit*, we had the idea of buying some sheet music for her. We found a small selection of Poulenc, Auric, Milhaud and Tailleferre piano pieces. They were the only ones of *Les Six* that we could find.

This year, Danielle had the inspiration to buy Natasha

a pair of lined black leather gloves.

"I hope we see her before May and it's too warm to wear them," Danielle said with a laugh.

ॐ

We saw Luke and Honorine on New Year's Day and had lunch with the Barnards – with far too much good wine. It was an especially joyous occasion as Honorine announced that she'd be having a baby in late May or early June.

"She's so vague about dates and times," Luc joked. "It will probably be October."

He had taken to working indoors fairly well, but would go out to supervise the unloading of the barrels and talk to his old colleagues whenever possible.

Simone was between boy friends (again) and had grown in confidence, and despite their age differences, she spent much of the time talking to Danielle.

Before we staggered home, we agreed to meet up and go to the cinema. A new film, *Marquitta*, was being talked about in the magazines, and Luc and Honorine were looking forward to it.

We were lucky that the next day was Sunday and we didn't have to drag ourselves to work.

XXXVII

Discovering Jazz

1927

After work on Thursday, Danielle and I went for a drink after work for the first time in the new year. Already, our plans had moved from the dream visions to the mundane.

"I've been carrying Natasha's gloves around all week and the wrapping is starting to look worn," she said. "I thought she might have materialised by now."

I thought the fact she hadn't was an indication that things were going well with Thomas, but Danielle was sceptical.

"Would you want a serious relationship with someone who never told you anything?" she asked. "Never mind what he might think about her various modelling and sleeping arrangements. I'm very fond of her and feel sorry for her, but she's really not the type of girl you'd want to take home to meet your family."

"And yet, you pay her rent," I countered.

She put her arm around me as we walked.

"Let's go see her," I said. "It's her Christmas eve. You can give her the gloves. If she goes to that freezing church tonight, she'll be glad of them."

The urgent work at the beginning of the year meant that we were unable to leave the office before seven all week. To make up for time, we took a taxi to Natasha's apartment and started up the stairs.

"Is every taxi driver in Paris Russian?" Danielle asked me as she paused after four floors.

"He was probably a prince," I said.

"If one believed such things, the presence of so many taxi drivers could provide a rather sinister system of spies," she whispered, though whether from fear of being overheard or breathless from the climb, I couldn't tell.

I laughed; it echoed in the stairwell so I, too, whispered.

"You should write to Gaston Leroux and suggest that it would be a good plot for his next sensational novel. A foreign intelligence department has infiltrated Parisian society through the city's taxi drivers, who not only provide information to the Okhrana, but carry out assassinations. . . ."

Danielle looked at me; I thought she actually looked worried.

"That's not funny, Charles," she said. "Not funny at all."

She raced ahead of me to the top of the building and waited for me outside Natasha's door.

We could hear voices inside; it sounded like a normal

discussion among students, with a few inflected exchanges followed by laughter.

We knocked and the door was opened by a young girl we hadn't seen before.

"We're friends of Natasha," Danielle said.

"One moment," she said, and closed the door.

"We must look like her parents," I said.

Danielle was still not pleased with me.

In a moment, Natasha opened the door, welcomed us and invited us in. Danielle had seen the apartment before, but I had not. It wandered over the whole top floor of the building. In some places the ceilings sloped at very sharp angles, and a hallway wandered through several turns from the entrance.

Natasha led the way passed the kitchen where five students sat around a table covered with books, papers, bottles, glasses and coffee cups.

"We can go in here," Natasha said.

We went into a small room that was used as a sitting room, and probably a spare bedroom for people unable to go home after a long evening.

Natasha looked wary, but was glad to see us.

"We came to wish you a happy Christmas," I said, and her face lit up.

"You remembered!"

"And we brought you a small present," Danielle said,

handing her the package.

Natasha seldom looked so joyful, and I hoped we could help keep her that way.

She carefully unwrapped the slim box and gave an unguarded exclamation in Russian, when she turned back the tissue paper. Her look of amazement as she removed a glove from the box and slipped it on her hand and admired it was out of all proportion to the present. She pushed her left sleeve and her tarnished bangle up her arm as she pulled on the other one.

Continuing to look at them, she flexed her fingers and the leather shone where it stretched.

"I – I must show Thomas!" she said, then called his name and started to the door.

Her call had an urgency that brought him to the doorway before she had left the room.

"Look!" she said, waving her hands before him.

He admired them, held her hands together in his and kissed her.

"Someone knows you well," he said to her, then smiled at us.

"I am blessed with some good friends," she replied.

"Apart from delivering the gloves and Christmas wishes, we were going to invite you for a meal. Would you like to join us, Thomas?" I asked.

Natasha looked suddenly sad.

"I am fasting before receiving the Holy Eucharist, and cannot eat or drink," she said. "I will leave shortly for Vespers and the Holy Liturgy. It's long, but beautiful."

Danielle must have looked disappointed as Natasha quickly added:

"But Thomas and I would love to join you tomorrow evening!"

We walked back down the stairs and realised how hungry we were by the time we reached the pavement.

There was no shortage of cafés, bistros and restaurants as we moved up Rue Monge to Boulevard Saint-Germain. We didn't know any of them, so picking one provoked some amusement and affectionate bickering. We eventually settled on the unprepossessing Bistro Bette which had a cosy look from the cold street, and more to the point, we could still see some empty tables.

When we had settled and were brought glasses of wine, we noticed that more people had been coming in and all the empty tables were filled. With the slight advantage, we were able to order before the newcomers.

"Do you think Natasha has found happiness?" I asked. "She hardly seemed the same girl."

Danielle turned her wine glass and stared at it.

"I thought she was still very thin," was all she was able to say before a curtain at the back of the room (which I had not noticed) opened and lights came up on a group of five musicians who immediately started playing popular songs but with instrumental elaborations.

We looked at each other, and Danielle gave one of her smiles that shed years from her face. She moved her head and shoulders in time to the music very subtly, and, for her, seductively. She then burst out laughing.

"It's called fun!" she said, loudly enough for me to hear.

And it was.

The unfettered life and enthusiasm made us believe that each musician loved what he was doing and that there was no place he would rather be. After a string of lively popular songs, a girl came out to join the musicians. She was dressed in a short but smart dress and had a jewelled headband with a feather.

She smiled at the audience as the band began playing a slow arrangement of "Someone to Watch Over Me." Her voice was dark and rich and held the room in silence. She sang two more moody songs before leaving the stage, and the band went back to playing "pacey" jazz.

When they took a break after nearly an hour of playing, Danielle reached across the table and took my hand.

"What a wonderful surprise this was," she said, her eyes sparkling with pleasure.

Indeed, it was fun to listen to popular music that didn't require much thought for a change.

During the break, we ordered desserts and were brought coffee just as the band reappeared. It played for another hour during which it was virtually impossible to speak. It played energetic pieces with each one featuring one of the musicians, among them, "Bye, Bye, Blackbird," "Has Anybody Seen My Girl," and "The Black Bottom Stomp," after which the singer returned to great applause and danced the "Charleston."

The final piece was an energetic rendition of "Show Me the Way to Go Home," after which they left the stage. They came back quickly for a curtain call, as some people were already preparing to leave, and took their places for an encore. As they began playing a long slow introduction, the singer returned and sang, "What'll I Do?"

Danielle continued to hum and sing snatches of it in the taxi on the way home as she leaned against me.

At least it was a French taxi driver, who will have understood.

XXXVIII
Different Rhythms

1927

Natasha met us at a bistro on Rue Soufflot. We'd expected her to bring Thomas and wondered why she hadn't. It was Friday, so he would not have pressing work.

"I wanted to talk without him," Natasha explained, taking off her gloves.

"Are things not going well?"

"Things are going very well," Natasha said. "We spend time together, but there isn't a lot. Medical students have a full programme, and he is also now doing art classes, too."

She laughed.

"I'm used to artists, but not ones like this," she said. "He is so methodical, patient, and works in such detail. He gets cross with me if I interrupt him."

"But it is Christmas for you," Danielle persisted. "Didn't he want to be with you – or you with him?"

She waved a hand then reached for her drink.

We ordered and Natasha told us about Midnight Mass.

"I was going to go to the Greek church, where I usually go, but, as you say, it's Christmas and that always makes me homesick. I needed to hear something familiar and comforting, even though it was a risk.

"I sat near the back, but not *at* the back, which would have attracted attention. I wanted to look good, but not too good, nor too poor," she said. "Nevertheless, I think I was noticed. There were ushers to help manage the crowd, and I am sure they were Okhrana. I was noticed, but they did not know who I was. That means they will continue to watch me, so I must be careful."

"You've hardly done anything this winter," I said. "You won't be able to do less."

She nodded.

"That's right," she said. "I must do more. I will go to *Kartofel* to see if I can work there a few days a week. As you saw, it is a place for peasants, not like the smart Russian tea rooms."

Our food came, and it occupied Natasha's full attention. Danielle and I continued to talk, but she did little more than nod.

"We neglected to thank you last night for the paintings. They're lovely," Danielle said. "Charles will hang them this weekend and you must come to see them."

"Do you not know anyone at a gallery who could sell these for you?" I asked. "You would get more from them than from a bookstall."

She put her knife and fork down and wiped her mouth.

"That would attract attention," she replied. "People would want to know who the artist was, where she studied, would she take commissions – I can't have any of that. Besides, I still have the problem of Thomas."

"How is Thomas a problem?" Danielle asked, not for the first time. "Is he not falling in love with you?"

When our coffee came, Natasha took out a cigarette. She was nervous and couldn't get the match to strike. I lit it for her, as Danielle gave me one of her knowing looks.

"We have fun," she said. "He's interesting, dedicated to his studies, and amusing; but, he is very inquisitive."

"That's normal, Natasha," Danielle said. "What do you expect?"

"He wants to know about my education, my family, what my father did, and worse, he wants to know what I did when I came to Paris."

Danielle was about to repeat her comment, but Natasha pressed on.

"What difference does it make what family or friends I had here, or what I did, or – "

"Natasha," I said, trying to soothe her. "Those are legitimate questions. Danielle and I asked hundreds of such questions. And don't worry, you'll both get answers that you might not like, but it's part of opening up to each other."

"I do not ask him such questions," Natasha said

defiantly. "What do I care what he did at school, or what the occupation of his father was?"

I think Danielle and I must have stared at her for too long as she shifted her attitude slightly.

"You think he's just curious?" she asked, less aggressively.

"He's not interrogating you, is he?"

She shrugged.

"It feels that way sometimes."

I sat back, and after a moment's silence, asked:

"So, what are you going to do?"

Natasha looked at us, and a look of resignation came over her face.

"If he is becoming serious, there are things I must tell him," she said. "I've had an idea, but don't know how it will work."

She paused and lit another cigarette while I ordered more coffee.

"I thought I would tell him in two parts," she said. "If he can accept the first part, I will tell him the second. If he doesn't like what he hears, I will not tell him the second part and he will be safe."

"And part one is – ?" Danielle asked.

"The part about modelling and living with divers artists and playing the piano at Madame Duflot's," she said.

"Does he not know you're playing there?" I asked.

"No," she mouthed, soundlessly.

"Well, young lady," Danielle began, "you are going to have to take your chances. Either you love and trust him enough to tell him, or he will find out from someone else – *and he will* – and it will be worse."

Natasha glanced at me for support, but I said that I thought Danielle was right, and she simply nodded.

o

It was several months before we saw Natasha again. We interpreted this as Thomas's acceptance of whatever she had told him and hoped they were happy.

Danielle and I revisited Bistro Bette and found several other cafés with good jazz. We met a few couples who frequented these hot spots and formed several lasting friendships. It was as a result of one couple that the four of us found ourselves at the Folies Bergère watching Josephine Baker. I can only endorse what others have said of her and note, decades later, that she was as charismatic as her reputation.

One Saturday afternoon in mid-April, Natasha found us at the Flamel. We were having a quick drink before going to the cinema.

Natasha looked disappointed when we told her we weren't going to eat, but Danielle invited her to join us, saying that we'd be eating after the film. While Danielle and I knew, Natasha had no idea just how far in the future that would be. The film was *Napoléon*, an incredibly long, but equally powerful film of Bonaparte's early life. It recently opened and was being shown at the *Théâtre National de l'Opéra.* We entered the theatre before mid-afternoon and came out at nine in the evening, stiff, tired, hungry and thoroughly amazed.

We were digesting the experience as we went to the restaurant and said little on the way. Once we'd decided on what to eat, we began talking about scenes and effects, many of which in our limited experience we had not seen before.

Natasha was quiet through most of the meal, but was attentive to our conversation. At the end she asked:

"When do you think people recognise they have a destiny?"

ભ

As we left the restaurant, Natasha suddenly remembered something.

"Keep May 21 free. There's a Koussevitzky concert that I am taking Thomas to. Meet us at the Opera at two-forty-five," she said and started to go.

"What will we be hearing?" I asked.

"Some new things and the Mussorgsky *Pictures.* I want to see his reaction, and I'd like you to be there, too."

Danielle nodded and the date was fixed.

Before we said good-night, Danielle exhorted her to be honest with Thomas and to move ahead without wasting time.

"Before the concert," Danielle said.

I thought it an unnecessary instruction, but trusted Danielle's insight.

"We'll see," Natasha replied, kissing her cheeks, and my optimism evaporated.

XXXIX
An Age of Wonders

1927

The crowds waited on the steps of the Opera until the last minute, not wishing to forego the sunshine and warm afternoon. We found Natasha and Thomas unceremoniously sitting on the steps and looking like the springtime lovers Paris is known for. She was wearing light colours which was unusual for her and looked younger and happy.

Danielle broke with her normal propriety and sat on the steps with them for a few moments before we made our way inside.

The first half comprised three new pieces: an overture by Prokofiev, a symphony by Alexandre Tansman, and a piece for harp by Germaine Tailleferre. *Pictures at an Exhibition* comprised the second half.

What Danielle and I noticed first was the relatively small number of Russians. Were they at work? Had they fallen out with Prokofiev or Koussevitzky? The auditorium was full and the performances excellent, with the Mussorgsky the undoubted high point; while enthusiastically received, it did not rival the near rapture we had witnessed five years earlier.

Inevitably, we thought of the chaotic scenes in the foyer and our march to *Kartofel*, and Fryderyka Gurin and Ilya, Count Viktorov. Vladimir was in Antibes with Gerald and Sara; the Rostovs were in London, and who knows who had replaced them. No one we saw looked familiar.

Thomas had been enthralled by the whole experience. As a scientist, he had seldom ventured into a concert hall, though his interest in anatomical drawing had taken him into the science museums and some galleries.

He had tried to describe how he felt at the end of the concert, but did it so badly that Natasha stopped him, laughing at his inarticulacy. I sympathised, having not that long ago been in his position.

"I've never heard anything like that," he said, laughing himself. "It was wonderful from beginning to end, and I finally understand what Natasha has been talking about."

He put his arm around her and pulled her close.

"You wait until she gets you to the ballet," I said.

"After that – whatever she wants!" he said.

"What I want is for you to say good-bye and to take me for something to eat," Natasha said, demonstrating more affectionate bantering than I'd seen.

She turned to us.

"We have things to talk about, otherwise, I'd invite you to join us."

"It might be fun with the four of us," Thomas began.

"Another time," Danielle said. "We'll look forward to it."

Natasha led him away.

"She's going to tell him after dinner," Danielle said.

"He's got to expect someone with her background – émigré or refugee – to have had a less conventional history than a student from Chartres," I said as we walked towards the river. "He seems a sensible *gars*, but it wouldn't be her past that would worry me."

Danielle stopped to face me.

"Do you really think she's in danger?" she asked.

"No; but I really think she's *un peu folle*, but probably not dangerous."

Danielle saw that I was serious and considered what I'd said.

"Do *you* think she's in danger?" I asked.

"I don't know, but things do seem to be happening around her."

"This new crowd she's taken up with sounds even stranger than the ones we saw at the Ballet Russes. Did she tell you about them? A bunch of Spaniards painting very odd stuff, according to Natasha. She loves it, of course. They sound like exhibitionists to me."

Danielle laughed, and we went home.

℘

It was a week later that we saw Natasha again. We, like thousands of other Parisians, had been astounded and excited by the news that someone had flown – single-handed – across the Atlantic. The American pilot had landed in Paris the night before and would be waving to the crowds from the Hotel de Ville. As it was a Sunday, we joined the mass of people walking down the street; there were so many of us that all other traffic was unable to move, much to the frustration of the drivers.

We waited with excited fellow citizens for nearly an hour when the first floor windows opened and a still tired but happy man stepped onto the ledge and waved. He was joined by a man waving a large American flag, and then by the American ambassador, whose difficulty in stepping up to the ledge made us wonder if he would not soon be lying in the street.

It was certainly the largest crowd that I had been in since my return to Paris after the Armistice was signed. It had all the buoyancy and bonhomie of that day with none of its sadness.

Danielle and I fell into conversation with an elderly man who was as excited as the youngest school boy present. He had been a professor of physics and told us he had long-predicted transatlantic aviation. Whether he had or not, he told us interesting things about the amount of fuel needed, the weight of the plane, navigational problems that pilots would encounter, air resistance at different altitudes, temperature differences and, of course, the need to stay awake and alert.

He might have been making it up, but it sounded convincing, and there was no mistaking his enthusiasm. The ambassador and the pilot stayed in the windows long enough that the crowd felt it had been worth it. There was not a lot for them to do up there except wave, and occasionally shake hands, while clinging to the mullion and trying not to look down.

When they eventually stepped down, the crowd cheered a few times to encourage another appearance, but there was only a wave from inside the room. We headed home along Rue de Temple, which was also overflowing with foot traffic.

Even with the crowds, we were home in a quarter of an hour and after walking and standing, we were looking forward to sitting down with a dish of tea. However, almost as soon as Danielle had shut the door, there was a knock on it.

When she opened it, Natasha virtually collapsed into her arms. She said nothing but clung to her until Danielle was able to manoeuvre her to the sofa where they sat next to each other.

Natasha continued to cling to her until Danielle freed herself.

"Now, Natasha; what is it? Are you hurt?" she asked gently.

"Mortally," she replied looking up.

Her eyes were puffy and bloodshot; she didn't look like she'd eaten since we last saw her.

I poured a *marc* and passed it to her. She took it and nodded, but did not drink.

Danielle waited while Natasha made a visible effort to become coherent. Putting the glass down, she pushed her hair back over her shoulders, straightened her dress, and momentarily closed her eyes. Then, she reached for the drink and took a small sip.

"That's more lethal than vodka," she said with a flicker of a smile.

She looked at both of us in turn.

"I'm finished," she said. "Thomas is gone, and the Okhrana has recognised me."

It took some time for the rest of her story to come out. When she and Thomas had left us after the concert, she and Thomas went for dinner. By her account, it was the sort of romantic evening that girls are said to dream of.

Then she chose to tell him about her departure from Russia and her years in Paris following the death of her guardian. He had listened without saying anything and when she had finished, he stood, threw a hundred francs on the table, and said that would cover dinner and his rent until the end of the month. When she returned from her session at Madame Duflot's he had left the apartment.

"You can't have been *that* bad," I said, and Danielle hit my arm. At least that made Natasha laugh. Then she looked at Danielle and said:

"I just didn't think he was so – *provincial!*"

~~From~~ *Natasha's Diary*

August 1927

This year is so different from last. Did I realise how happy I was then? I see my destiny is the common Russian one: partly my own fault, and partly the grinding course of our history. How is it that the French, even with their recent, crushing losses can emerge with such vitality, while all my countrymen in Paris have brought their misery with them?

After Thomas left, I spent most of the time I was not working walking along the streets that had once made me happy. I was in Rue de l'Odéon near the bookstore where the English and American writers gather when the Irishman saw me, and greeted me as "Madame X." That seems so long ago. He has done some wonderful things since then and over a drink, he showed me sketches of a new bronze of Tristan and Isolde, which I found very moving.

We talked of various artists, but he seemed not to be impressed with the ones I knew. He said I could find him through M. Hébrard and that when he had finished Tristan at the beginning of next year, he might have some work for me.

It was during these walks that I saw the men who I have seen before at concerts, galleries, restaurants, Oleg's funeral and elsewhere. They've never said anything, but somehow they know me, and I know it cannot be long.

I will write what I can for Charles and Danielle so they will finally understand.

Sandra is now married and very happy; not living with her mother has been good for her. She continues to cook for Mademoiselle, and her food is better than ever.

Before coming to Gargenville this year, I worked very hard; I did not want to disappoint Mademoiselle in what I fear will be my last time. She seems pleased, but senses something is wrong; she says she can tell by the way I play Tchaikovsky, so she has given me three preludes by Gershwin to help my mood. While within my technical ability, they are not in my character – "Then change your disposition," Mademoiselle says. I wish I could.

I have not had to go to the bank in the last year. It is Danielle's generosity that has made that possible, so maybe it is enough to last for the rest of my life.

It was only supposed to last until I was married.

XL
La Bella Donna

1927

At the beginning of October when we hadn't heard from Natasha, Danielle suggested we go to her apartment on the Saturday.

"If I'm paying rent, I want to be sure she's living there and hasn't eloped to Barcelona with a sur-realist," she said.

"If that draws a blank, we can try the Ballet Russes," I said. "Someone there might recognise us."

We were still in the post-holiday period of catching up and after working long weeks were having quiet week-ends, so there had been no events that would have warranted contacting Natasha.

We had been to the cinema but the first time we went, once settled in the dark, we both fell asleep. The second attempt was more successful and *Le Mystère de la Tour Eiffel* was intriguing enough to keep us awake.

We were still at work on Friday, 8 October, when just after six o'clock, Luc Barnard knocked on our office door.

"I am sorry to bother you at work," he said, after we greeted him. "I have some bad news."

We immediately thought of his parents, then his baby

son, but he impatiently thanked us and said they were all fine.

"It's about Mlle Tarasova," he said. "I'm sorry, but. . . she's dead."

Danielle and I looked at each other blankly.

"Ilya's friend; Natasha?" he said. "I didn't really know her."

I put my arm around Danielle and held her tightly. We stared, uncomprehending, at Luc trying to absorb the news.

"Sit down," Danielle said.

"What happened?" I asked, once we were all seated.

"I still talk to the bargees," he explained. "There are still a lot who I know. Sometimes I even travel with them a short distance and take the train back to Paris. Ilya was only one of quite a few Russians on the boats, and, as you know, if they're not close, there's a web of connections.

"She was pulled out of the Seine near Saint Denis Tuesday night. I'm sorry," he added, noticing the tears on Danielle's cheeks.

"What else do you know?" I asked, my own voice barely audible.

"She didn't drown," he said, and we both looked up sharply. "The police said it looked like she was poisoned. As luck would have it, the dock manager who spotted her body had an uncle who was a doctor. They both waited for the police and he told them he didn't think she had drowned. You get these Russians and suicide is not uncommon."

"Is there someone we can contact? There ought to be a funeral," I said.

"The Sûreté should be able to tell you if anyone claimed the body."

Neither of us was able to concentrate on anything else. We thanked Luc, and I took Danielle home.

"Go to the police. Now!" she said when we got home. "We owe her that."

I went to the local police and asked where such information would be held and was directed to the Quai des Orfèvres.

At first, they were reluctant to give me any information as I had to look at a piece of paper to remember the name Tarasova. I explained that even though I'd known her for many years, she was secretive and never told me her last name.

A young constable made a rude suggestion that it was like knowing someone called "Fifi," but he was sharply rebuked by the duty sergeant.

"If no one has claimed the body, my wife and I would like to," I said.

After a few minutes a police detective in plain clothes came down and escorted me to an office on the third floor, where I met a more senior inspector. I related much of the history of how we'd known Natasha. (I didn't want anymore rude suggestions and made sure he understood that she was an old friend to both of us).

He confirmed that her death was being treated as murder, but that there was little hope of finding anyone. He said that a detective named Lapin was actively looking into the case.

"He's young, but a good officer," the inspector said. "He's thorough and, frankly, would love to prove himself on this case. He will do all he can for Mlle Tarasova."

I believed him; the fact that he'd even remembered Natasha's name told me that the police were taking her murder seriously.

"Do you believe the Okhrana still exists?" I dared to ask.

His expression provided all the answer I needed.

"M. Boivet," he began, "I will be pleased to give you the details of the gentleman who claimed the body, and suggest you contact him, or the authorities at the Russian church for information about the funeral and burial arrangements.

"But, please, *for your own safety*, do not pursue any private inquiries about the former organisation you mentioned."

He was polite, but emphatic. His tone was enough to

frighten me more than anything Natasha had told us, and I had no inclination to disobey this instruction.

He gave me the name and address of Vasily Kristoff. I had an address for his office, which meant I could do nothing more until Monday. I thanked the inspector for his patience and help and went home.

Danielle physically shuddered when I repeated the inspector's warning about Okhrana.

"Promise me, Charles," she said, imploring me in a way she had never done, "*Never* utter that word again."

I agreed and showed her the paper with Kristoff's name on it and said I'd visit him Monday morning.

"I have a better idea," she said. "We'll go to the cathedral tomorrow. If we can't find him, we might be able to get details of the funeral."

Apart from recalling some of the adventures we'd had together, there was little more to be done until morning.

໖

We estimated that if we arrived at the Alexandre Nevsky Cathedral by noon, the ten o'clock Mass would just about be over. We entered the church when people began coming out.

Danielle was able to find someone who looked like an usher and within a few moments was pointed to a man identified as Vasily Kristoff. I judged him to be younger than I, which gave me a little more confidence as we approached him, but it was Danielle who spoke first."

"M. Kristoff, may we please have a word with you about Natasha Tarasova."

It was a command, not a request.

We introduced ourselves as friends of Natasha's who had been shocked and saddened to learn of her death. Kristoff indicated empty chairs to the side and we sat down.

"Did you know her?" Danielle asked.

"Not personally, but as you may know, members of the White Russian community are aware of each other. Mlle Tarasova knew many of us, mostly through the Ballet Russes."

Danielle kept squeezing my hand to stop me from challenging him.

"Where is she now?" I asked.

"She is with an undertaker who is known to the community. She will be properly prepared for the funeral Wednesday," he said. "Will you be able to attend?"

"Absolutely," Danielle said.

"Where will she be buried?" I asked.

"There is a cemetery south of Paris in Sainte Geneviève-des-Bois," he said. "Many Russians are buried there."

I sensed that Danielle was going to ask who was paying, so it was my turn to squeeze her hand to stop her. No sense in looking like volunteering.

"It will all be done properly," he said. "Madame Goncharova is making her burial dress."

We must have looked puzzled, so he explained.

"Have you ever been to a Russian funeral?"

"We went to Ilya's; Count Viktorov's."

Kristoff nodded.

"This will be a little different, and it's best you know before you are upset," he explained. "Count Viktorov's coffin was closed because of his wound; usually they are open.

"Natasha will be dressed in an unfinished white dress – it won't have hems and other such things. It is to show that she is no longer of this world. She will probably be wearing a red belt, that signifies vitality and life. What you will find curious is that there will be a paper band around her head. In Russian will be written 'Holy God, Holy Mighty, Holy Immortal, have mercy on us.'

"There will be a chance to walk up and see her, and kiss her, if you want; as good friends, you may wish to, though nothing is mandatory," he said with a slight smile. "Other rituals you will find similar to the Roman Rite: oil and earth will be sprinkled in the coffin and the priest will then pull up the shroud.

"I hope you feel welcome; you will no doubt see some familiar faces. After the burial, there will be a reception which you are also welcome to attend."

He sounded very compassionate and seemed to take pride in the adherence to traditional rituals.

"It sounds well organised," Danielle ventured.

"It is one of the Union's services," he said.

XLI
Love Endures Forever

1927

We were contented when we left the cathedral. Kristoff had been charming, sensitive and sympathetic. Yet, the more he spoke, the more he seemed to know about Natasha, and we wondered how. By the time we were home, I was suspicious, and Danielle nearly terrified.

"It seems that I don't know my own city," she said. "Everything Natasha said was true. I'm not sure I want to be with those people. Kissing corpses is barbaric and unsanitary; I hope you don't expect me to do it."

I thought it strange, but a beautiful way to say goodbye to someone you hadn't been able to in life. When it came time, I hoped I had the courage.

After lunch, she was more objective and calm, but the realisation that Natasha had not merely been fantasising, as we had long told ourselves, disturbed us.

On Wednesday, shortly after ten-thirty, dressed in mourning, we went to the Rue Daru, and taking a deep breath, entered the cathedral. We could immediately see the coffin with Natasha partly covered in a white shroud. There were bunches of flowers at her sides. We took places at the back where we had been for Ilya's funeral. This was mostly so we didn't see her too closely, as I don't think either of us could have borne it. It was also a good place for watching people enter, and, as Kristoff had predicted, we recognised a number of people, including Koussevitzky, which surprised us. We didn't know the names of many, but recognised them from the set painting at the ballet, or the crowd at *Kartofel*. These people had faces that you didn't forget. We were surprised to see Vladimir Orloff, whom we had supposed to be on the Riviera. Then it seemed that a sea of black came in all at once, Madame Goncharova led them, and Diaghilev followed with much of the stage crew from the Ballet Russes. We wouldn't have recognised the dancers, but assumed some were there, too. The other person we recognised was "Mademoiselle," who looked deeply grieved as she made her way up the aisle.

A minute before eleven o'clock, bells started to ring, and the funeral began. Ancient rituals take on a life of their own; there is the momentum of the ages to help people from grief to hope, if one can but let it.

While bits of the service were recognisable, there was no Communion. We understood nothing of what was said by the priest, but the odd word led me to believe that it was a theological message rather than anything to do with Natasha.

When the time came, joining the line to pay the final respects to Natasha seemed very natural. She looked so tiny in her coffin and was nearly overwhelmed by the flowers. Her luxuriant auburn hair was carefully arranged, and she looked at peace in a way that she had not in life.

Danielle tells me that my face was streaming with tears when I returned to my seat.

It was the only time I had kissed her.

ɛɔ

We had decided not to go to the cemetery. Everyone would be speaking in Russian, and we felt we had done what we could. Perhaps we'd visit the grave later.

We stood on the steps with the crowd and watched the coffin carried with the greatest care to the hearse and waited for it to depart. While standing there, I noticed another figure, who, like us, stood apart from the other mourners. It was the Irishman. I hadn't seen him since the opening at Galerie Hébrard, what seemed a lifetime ago.

I moved to him.

"Your *Madame X*," I said. "I saw it when it was first shown. It's where I met Natasha."

"If that was her name," he replied. "I never knew for certain."

We didn't feel like going to work but decided to go to a café near one of the parks, eventually ending up at

325

Angelina in the Rue de Rivoli. Without tourists, it was easy to get a table. We weren't particularly hungry and just had tea with a few *sablés*.

"Whether she liked the organisers or not, that was quite a funeral," Danielle said, after having sat quietly for a few minutes. "I found Ilya's funeral moving, and I didn't know him; this – I don't know – made me feel I was actually near the gates of heaven."

I reached to take her hand.

"No," she said softly, drawing it away. "I don't think I could take kindness just now."

"It was ironic that someone who was trying to stay out of sight had nearly two hundred people at her funeral," I said. "I wish I knew who was there – and why."

Danielle shook her head.

"No. Natasha warned us about being curious," she said. "Please, Charles, let's just remember her and the things we did together."

ଓଃ

We returned to work, and our ordinary lives soon made the memories of Natasha fade. We continued to find places to listen to jazz, and we went to the cinema a few times a month. At some of the places where jazz was played, we also danced a little.

We did not go to concerts or galleries for some time; we both knew that we'd look for Natasha in the crowd.

Indeed, even at meals at the Flamel, when the door opens, I look up to see if she is entering.

One day during Lent in 1928, we decided it would be good for us to try to visit Natasha's grave. We knew we wouldn't find it on our own, so we would have to go when the cemetery would be attended.

One Wednesday, we left work shortly after eleven and went to Gare Austerlitz and boarded a train to Sainte-Geneviève-des-Bois. Danielle had bought some flowers which she carried carefully and looked at for most of the journey. We took a taxi to the Russian cemetery and were able to find someone who led us to her grave. We had neglected to consider the problems of reading Cyrillic.

It was pretty much like all the others and simply said, *"Наташа Тарасова, 1903 – 1927,"* with an Orthodox cross carved below it. The letters were well cut, but not picked out with gold paint, she wouldn't have liked that.

Danielle placed her flowers and we said a few prayers. The caretaker may have been curious about the two Papists who had come to his cemetery, but he said nothing. I asked him where Ilya was buried, and he gave the slightest acknowledgement that we knew something about the Parisian Russians. He was less than sixty feet away in the same alley as Natasha. His stone was grander of black marble and the lettering was picked out in gold. All that was carved were his name, dates and the cross; no acknowledgement of his service, or his rank. After a few moments, we turned to go, ensuring that we tipped the caretaker. He smiled and said a few words in Russian, and we left.

While we still had questions, we didn't ask them. We weren't close to anyone else in that community, and it felt like the end of an adventure. The girl we knew as Natasha was dead, and we had lives to lead.

XLII

Some Answers, More Questions

September 1928

Moreau, Doré et Cie continued to thrive and as Danielle took on more management responsibilities, our expansion continued. It was not a large company, but it was several times bigger than when I had joined. The liveliness of Paris continued unabated, but the unexpected is never distant.

It had just passed five o'clock on a Thursday afternoon when one of our clerks knocked on our door to say we had a visitor. I went to the front office and found Thomas standing there looking very nervous.

"May I please speak with you and Mme Boivet?" he asked. "But, not here."

I looked at the clock on the wall.

"It's very important."

I told him to wait for us at the *Café L'Hommes d'Affairs* and that we'd be there at six. He seemed happy with this proposal, and I went to tell Danielle.

She sank back in her chair.

"*Please, no.*"

I sat back down at my desk and said nothing and pretended to do some work.

"Do you know what he wanted?" Danielle eventually asked.

"He looked very nervous. I think he was afraid I was going to hit him."

"I don't know if I want to re-open those memories just yet," she said.

"He asked to see both of us," I said, still checking orders. Pushing her was not going to get her to comply.

She worked a few more minutes and took a phone call, and I continued to work.

"I suppose we should hear what he has to say," she said. "There might be some happy memories to share."

Thomas was even more uneasy when we arrived. He stood and formally shook hands with us, then asked us if we'd like a drink and ordered a bottle of red.

"You must think me a cruel cad," he began. "I know that's how it looks, and I will not try to defend myself, except to say that I am the first person in my family to be able to come to Paris to study. To be a doctor will be a landmark for my family, and begin to repay what my parents have done for me."

We said nothing, but Danielle gave him an encouraging nod.

"We are very ordinary, very conventional people," he said apologetically. "People and things who are unconventional seem to threaten us. Natasha called me 'provincial,' which was about as damning as she could get, but she stopped short of calling me a peasant, which would have been justified."

He was beginning to panic, so I interrupted.

"What can we do for you?"

The arrival of our drinks forestalled his reply, though we did not drink.

"I have been visiting the police every week to see if there had been progress in their investigation," he said. "They had nothing to go on, and have now stopped actively trying to find a – perpetrator."

He reached to the side of his chair and produced a large brown envelope, secured with string and a wax seal.

"These were Natasha's," he said, handing it over. "She came to see me when she returned from Gargenville, that summer. She told me that as much as it hurt, she still thought fondly of me and wished me success and good fortune."

He appeared close to tears, but, again, it was my surprising wife who interceded.

"I don't think Natasha ever wished anyone harm," she said, and he nodded.

"The last thing she said to me was, 'Love in action is a harsh and dreadful thing compared to love in dreams.' I think she was quoting something," he said shaking his head.

He said nothing for a moment and I suspected that Danielle was losing patience with him.

"She said if anything happened to her, I should give this to you," he said. "I had given it to the police and they gave it back to me today. It's yours, so I asked them to re-seal the envelope; I haven't looked at the contents. I don't know if the police found anything significant inside, they didn't tell me. I presume everything is there."

I took the envelope and showed it to Danielle.

"*Les effets de TARASOVA Natasha, 12 Rue du Cardinal Limoine, V. Le 11 Octobre 1927,*" was all it said.

Thomas had displayed dedication in his determination to find out what had happened to Natasha. He had made a nuisance of himself to the police until the detective began to trust him. He also had some luck: as a medical student he had heard a lecture by the coroner who had examined Natasha and was able to speak to him with the consent of the inspector. Also on his side was the young detective's ambition; he had immediately suspected this was not suicide.

"I shouldn't have left her," he said, miserably. "I did love her."

"She was an unusual person, Thomas," I said. "She wasn't easy; even with those who were used to her ways. Tell me what you learned."

"Professor Dr Morriseau gave me five minutes, and that was because I was with Detective Lapin," he said. "The professor was impressed with Lapin who had taken the time to *look* and raise his suspicions.

"Did you see the autopsy report?" Thomas asked.

Danielle covered her mouth and Thomas quickly backtracked.

"I'm sorry," he said. "I'm more used to this, but believe me, when I think of this in connection with Natasha, it makes me weep."

Danielle drank some wine, and took a deep breath.

"No, Thomas," she said. "If you think that knowing these things will give us any comfort or understanding, tell us."

I glanced at her, but she was looking directly at Thomas.

"Detective Lapin requested the autopsy," he began. "He had seen what is called petechial haemorrhaging in her eyes as well as dilated pupils. Petechial haemorrhaging is like having very badly bloodshot eyes and it is extremely uncommon in drowning."

"Wasn't there a doctor there when she was recovered?" I asked.

"Yes," he nodded. "He had focused on seeing if her mouth was obstructed and then mechanically trying to revive her. He had only begun when the police arrived but he believed that there was not a great quantity of water in her lungs. I don't know how he deduced this. Probably by the resistance of her rib-cage, or perhaps the resonance of her chest cavity."

I had seen all kinds of death, and looked at Danielle who was listening with interest. Thomas's gentle manner was quietly confident and was not upsetting her.

"There were no bruises on her body; no signs of a struggle which can suggest suicide," he said. "However, the autopsy revealed a significant quantity of *bella donna* in her stomach, including ground leaf material, suggesting it was mixed into the strawberry jam also found, along with tea and a remains of a *sablé*."

"Her tea!" Danielle exclaimed. "Poor girl!"

"To be certain – and to set my own mind at rest - I asked if it still might have been suicide," Thomas continued. "The professor said no, rather emphatically. There was, he said, enough belladonna in her system to have made death fairly rapid. He said that she would have barely made it out of the room where she'd drunk her tea.

"The professor also agreed with Lapin that whoever had given her the poisoned jam probably waited for her outside and took her to the river," he said sadly. "Since she'd drifted down stream, there's no way of knowing where she went in. The café itself may have been one or two streets from the Seine. There were no other reports of similar poisonings, so that's as far as it can be taken."

He sank back, looking bereft of energy.

I nodded at the unhappy young man.

"You've' done well, Thomas," I said. "It was murder – perhaps assassination – who knows?"

He nodded, thoughtfully, and stood to go.

"What made you visit the police so often?" I asked, still curious about his tenacity.

"I felt guilty. Even with the results, I still feel guilty," he said miserably, sitting back down. "If I had been with her more, she might have been safe."

"Young man!" Danielle said, loudly enough for the people at the next table to look, "That sort of talk is morbid. I think Charles and I know that the forces against the girl we knew as Natasha were far greater than any of us could have protected her from."

Both Thomas and I were jolted by her outburst.

"As for you," she continued, "you may have acted in a cowardly way, but you did so with good reason, and you could not have predicted what happened, nor prevented it.

"Remember your good times," she went on, gently. "Laugh about how exasperating she could be and *never* be ashamed of loving her."

Her last words were whispered and left us in

momentary silence.

Suitably chastened, Thomas took his glass and raised it.

"Natasha."

He drank it, and we wished him success in his studies.

"Thank you, Thomas," Danielle said. "You know where we are, and you will always be welcome."

Back at our apartment, the envelope sat on our dining table.

"Let's eat first," Danielle said. "I doubt we'll be hungry after opening that."

XLIII
Disclosures

When we finished the meal we had little appetite for, I fetched the envelope and put it on the table before us. We still had a good part of a bottle to finish, and I filled our glasses.

We both stared at it, wondering what, if anything, it would change. Finally, I broke the seal, opened the envelope and slid the contents out onto the table.

There were probably fifty sheets of paper, some in Russian, some in French, about fifteen watercolours on good paper, and the sheet music we had given her one Christmas. There was also a small Russian prayer book, a silver Russian crucifix, and the dark metal bangle that she always wore.

These were the remains of twenty-four years of life.

We set aside the watercolours, the prayer book and the jewellery, and turned to the handwritten pages.

The handwriting was strong and even, and we found that the few pages in Russian had French translations written on the back.

We leafed through them, casually looking at her reflections while in Gargenville (reproduced above). The final document, although dated as the other pages, was in the form of a letter, and as we read it, we realised it was a letter to us.

21 August [1927]
Gargenville

This is my last night at Mademoiselle's. It has been good, but I remain troubled and have not shaken my unease.

I still sometimes cry that Thomas could not accept me, but I do understand. He is young and has not yet had the experiences that make one tolerant, though he is basically kind. Should you see him, let him know that he mostly made me happy.

There is really only one circumstance in which you will read any of this, so let me start, my dear Charles and Danielle, by thanking you. You have been generous and kind to someone who could offer you very little. You went along with my impulses – and I hope enjoyed some of them – and on occasion, tried to rein me in. For all of that, I thank you.

Over the years, I have sensed that Charles has wondered what ever prompted him to ask me to dinner that night, or for what possible reason I accepted. It certainly set into motion some unexpected events.

In truth, I cannot answer that. I sensed you were someone who was not like the other people I knew in

338

Paris: you didn't expect anything. You certainly didn't expect to marry Danielle, but that's how life is.

It would be easy for me to have lots of regrets and bitterness. I certainly have regrets, not so much for myself, but for my country, my family, and so many of my friends. I am happy for Anya and André who lost so much, but kept each other. Those who escape – and survived escaping – have much to be thankful for.

The revolutionaries didn't just take our country, they took who we are, and that is what has made it so difficult to find our way again.

One of my regrets is that I was unable to tell you about myself. You both wanted to know my story; at first, I was suspicious, but I came to know that you wanted me to tell you to help you understand me. I could not risk it; I could not risk you getting hurt, but now it is safe and I can tell you.

My mother is still alive, though she has probably presumed me dead for a long time. Her name was Beatrice of Saxe-Coburg and Gotha. As a grand-daughter of Queen Victoria, she is a princess. Shortly after the turn of the century, she met and fell in love with my father, but because she was Church of England and he was Russian Orthodox, the British royal family would not sanction their marriage. Nonetheless, I was born, illegitimately, in 1903. As Danielle guessed, I was well-educated and brought to

Paris in 1916, when the writing was on the wall.

Ironically, my mother married into the Spanish royal family and converted to Roman Catholicism, so what was the point of the earlier objection? The perspective of a decade and the Great War changed things, I suppose.

After the Revolution, my guardian's money stopped, and, fearing her own life, she escaped to the United States. Since then, I've done what I could to live and remain inconspicuous. That was the beauty of working for Madame Duflot; if someone recognised me – and the chances of that were slender – they wouldn't dare say where they'd seen me.

However, it wasn't knowledge of my mother who presented the danger but that of my father.

His name was Michael Alexandrovich Romanoff, youngest brother of Nicholas II, and according to some, the last tsar.

Do what you will with this knowledge; you do not have to protect me any more, but do not endanger yourselves.

The small cross which I hope has come to you was given to me by my parents at my birth, and the bracelet was from my father, given to me when I fled Russia. I called it "my bank."

I pray that your lives are long and safe, and thank you from the heart.

Alexandra Mikhailovna Romanova
(Madame X)

∞

It was some time before we could face speaking about this and look more closely at the documents, paintings and objects. Danielle made me put them out of sight to keep her from bursting into tears. Even so, she would occasionally spontaneously say out loud, "That poor girl."

It was the beginning of Advent when we decided that we'd be able to look at *les effets de Natasha Tarasova* again. In the meantime I had visited a library and found that the names and dates Natasha had given us were accurate. Accidentally, I found that the statue referred to in her account of her last meeting with the Irishman had won him the Grand Prix of the Paris Salon in 1928. We had not visited it.

One evening, I leafed through Natasha's watercolours again. I thought they were pleasing and was very glad to have them. As I did this, Danielle looked closely at the bangle which she had not been able to face touching.

It was dirty, tarnished and had not a small amount of what we supposed was scenery paint on it, but it could have come from her artists. Danielle picked at it with her fingernail for a bit, then went to the kitchen for a rag and some polish.

The bangle was about three-quarters of a centimetre

wide with a very gentle curve in its surface. Glancing at Danielle, it appeared to be polishing up.

"*Mon Dieu!*" she suddenly exclaimed and gave it to me while she went to fetch something else.

It was silver, but what had startled her was that the inside of the bangle was set with stones. As I turned it, it looked like every other stone was missing, except in one section, three in a row were gone.

Danielle returned with a magnifying glass, a ramekin of ammonia, and a wooden skewer.

"This is why she called it her bank," she said. "Twelve stones that were virtually hidden, one to be removed when she needed money."

She took the bangle carefully from the liquid, wiped it dry and scraped a section with the stick.

"These are diamonds!"

It was her survival equipment and her dowry. Danielle continued to work on it until most of the surface paint was gone; cleaning the settings and the stones would be a job for a jeweller.

"Look!" she said again and pointed to the edge of the bracelet.

What appeared to be a dent was in fact a small flat area where there was a mark. Looking through the glass, we could read, but not understand, the word:

ФАБЕРЖЕ

Epilogue

1969

Does anyone even care any more?

The departure of our president has prompted me to pull these recollections together, and I've nothing else to do.

In the heady days of the late 1920s did we have any idea how near the precipice we were? The financial collapse controlled our lives for the next decade and after that, the Nazis.

Somehow, we managed to survive, even both Danielle's parents and mine, but those years exhausted them, and once they could visualise a more peaceful future, they decided to leave the world to others. They were all dead by 1950. No long illnesses, DG; no traumatic accidents, just a winding down and closing up.

Danielle and I, and Jules Moreau, who is considerably younger than we are, managed to keep the company running until 1960 when there was a good opportunity to sell it.

Danielle (who had for some time been passing herself off as younger than I) and I were in good health and in our early sixties at the time of the sale. We were able to travel but our ambitions were not excessive.

Not having been born for greatness, we simply continued to enjoy each other's company, visit old friends, and enjoy meals together.

Over time, we gave Thomas two of Natasha's watercolours, and another two to Luc and his sister. The "bank" remains in a box at the back of Danielle's bureau. At least I think it does. She keeps it with a bottle of nail varnish in case she ever decides to run away.

Once in a while at a party or in a bar at a resort hotel, someone mentions a name from the past. Mentioning that we were once at a party with Picasso and Stravinsky is usually worth a few drinks, but this is rare. Our daughter, now just under forty, only recently discovered that her mother had painted costumes with Natalia Goncharova and questioned her about it intensely.

"Why haven't you told me this before?" she demanded. "What else don't I know?"

One day, she'll find out.

She'll also find out why her middle name is Alexandra; we couldn't bear to call her Natasha. She'll also discover that she'll inherit a small, silver bangle and an Orthodox cross.

Danielle and I seldom talk about the 1920s, unless it's to tell how our relationship grew and flourished. It's not that we view them with sadness; it's not because what came afterwards was so painful for so long; and, it's not wholly because people don't care.

It's mostly because they wouldn't believe it if we told them.

So, we bicker about whether *croissants* are as good as they used to be, if Paris still smells as sweet, and who got jam on *Le Figaro*.

Les années folles were times of excess and turmoil, and many lives were subsequently ruined, *mais, mon Dieu, comme le jazz était superbe!*

Charles Boivet

Fin

Acknowledgements

My thanks to friends and strangers who helped me with my research and writing.

Julie Dexter for proof-reading, editing, encouragement and suggestions for improvements.

The Very Reverend Father John J Matusiak, who helps to maintain the excellent Orthodox Church in American (oca.org) website for information on Russian Orthodox practices.

Kerry Scott, composer and writer, for suggesting the possibilities for the Glazunov Violin Concerto No. 2.

Ian Thomson, author of *The Northern Elements*, for untangling my French.

Dr. Victor Yuzefovich, musician, author and Koussevitzky authority, who offered a realistic explanation for the advance programme notice announcing a performance of the *Deuxième Conceto pour Violon* by Glazunov on 6 May 1921.

By the same author:

Undivulged Crimes

What do you really know about the person sitting next to you? The tales in *Undivulged Crimes* encompass the romantic, ghostly, satiric, and the simply disturbing. Set in the United States and Europe, these stories explore secrets from the dark side of ordinary people, from an historical curse, to fraud, deceit, and murder.

On the Edge of Dreams and Nightmares

A tale of child-abuse, incest, madness and murder: Ligeia Gordon's solution to her deep psychological troubles is to infiltrate the life of the distinguished painter, Sir Nigel Thomas, an older man who has his own ghosts to contend with.

Winner of A Chill With A Book Premier Award.

Portland Place: A novel from Jane Austen's Lost Years

Jane Austen meets the Americans. In the early 1800s, Nora Woodruff finds herself in London for the first time, and encountering citizens of the new nation. Manners and attitudes conflict against a background of rising political tension.

The Countess Comes Home

At the end of the Vietnam War, Lieutenant (j.g.) Bill Bradley is ordered to deliver documents from Yankee Station to Saigon, to an enigmatic young woman he knows only as "the countess." Decades later, the shadow of that mission falls on his retirement when a message is received saying that the countess wants to return to London.

Entrusted in Confidence

Bill Bradley, Sir Julian Osgood and the countess make return appearances in three pendant stories to *The Countess Comes Home*. "The Countess's Secret", "The Brentano Affair", and "Bill Bradley Rides Again" deliver their characteristic mix of espionage, intrigue and wry humour against a background of contemporary events.

Nantucket Summer

From the haunted residents of the darkened rooms of the unpainted Hardwicke mansion, Midwestern waitresses, and the retreats of the establishment, to the creeping, *nouveau riche* infiltrators with their oversized, post-modern houses and competitive spirits, *Nantucket Summer* is a memoir of those who summered on the wood-framed New England coast in the 1960s.

348

Wachusett

In the summer of 1876, the nation prepares to mark its centennial. Marion Easton travels from her Boston home to a resort hotel on Mount Wachusett in central Massachusetts where she joins her future in-laws and their family. However, as July 4 approaches, there is little to celebrate.

The Camels of the Qur'an

The death of a BBC journalist, a missing girl, and an unpublished novel, lead the reluctant David Powell into a labyrinth of Middle Eastern customs, politics and intrigue. Determined to discover if his friend's death was an accident, or murder, Powell finds his familiar reference points gone, and nothing quite what it seems.

Watch for:

The Rock Pool

The power of a special place can become a lasting influence, and when combined with the experience of love, it is a potent mix. Nick Lucas's love for the unobtainable Sarah Hallam becomes the unwelcome centre of his life.

edit upload 16 July 2020.

Printed in Great
Britain
by Amazon

31091070R00213